D1161731

# Matt Monroe and the Haunted House

# MATT MONROE AND THE HAUNTED HOUSE

EDWARD TORBA

**Matt Monroe and The Haunted House**

1st Edition



Published by: All Points Press
ISBN 978-0-9850827-8-9 (Hardback)
ISBN 978-0-9850827-6-5 (Paperback)
ISBN 978-0-9850827-7-2 (eBook)

Printed in the United States
Cover Design by S.C. Watson, www.oreganoproductions.com
Interior Design by The Deliberate Page, www.DeliberatePage.com

*This book is dedicated to all of you who have been bullied at school, on the playground, or anywhere else.*

*Payne Mansion, present day*

# CONTENTS

PROLOGUE

# Midnight Mayhem

*October, 1901…*

It was a gloomy night, one that could sour even the most hopeful soul. The moon hung low over the murky woods, playing a sinister game of hide-and-seek with the hovering clouds in the night sky, while a cold breeze blew through the tall maples and poplars. The trees' oddly bent limbs shook and swayed rhythmically to the hypnotic tune of the chilly wind. This created ghostly shadows that danced on the narrow path below, menacing apparitions ready to reach out and snatch anyone who dared enter this forsaken place.

Their scraped, bare feet stumbled over exposed tree roots, as the boy urged his little sister to run faster, following a twisted path that led to an uncertain end. Nathaniel pulled Annabelle over a fallen log. Behind them, the sound of heavy footsteps crashed through the blanket of dry leaves, interrupting the wind's spellbinding song.

Confused by the darkness, Nathaniel scurried blindly through the forest. He'd explored this maze of trees many times in the safety of daylight, but never so late at night.

Nathaniel whispered urgently to his sister, "Keep moving. You saw what he did to Mama."

Annabelle whined as she struggled to keep up. She sniffled; tears ran down her cheeks. "I need to rest."

"We can't stop." He picked up his sister and held her close to his chest. "You have to be brave."

The boy wrapped his arms around the tiny girl's waist in an attempt to carry her, but his young limbs were not strong enough to bear the weight. Although he gave it his best effort, Nathaniel couldn't maintain his balance. He took a few steps, then staggered and fell. Their entangled bodies plunged down a steep hillside. They rolled and slid until stopped by a clump of trees that cradled them in their gnarled roots.

Loud footsteps came from the path above, then halted abruptly. A dark figure stood motionless on the narrow trail and peered in the direction of brother and sister, who lay hidden in the darkness.

A deep male voice shouted urgently, "Nathaniel! Annabelle!"

The distressed man veered off the path and ventured so close, Nathaniel could hear his heavy breathing and could actually smell the garlic on the man's breath.

"Come out now, and I'll forget you disobeyed me."

Annabelle whimpered. Nathaniel covered her mouth and cuddled her trembling body.

The dark figure stood directly above them.

Nathaniel quivered, sure they'd been spotted. He tried to be strong for his sister, but his heart pounded and the queasiness he felt in the pit of his stomach intensified. He feared the severity of the punishment he would receive if they were caught.

The troubled man grunted, and then came a repeated fierce stomping that terrified Nathaniel.

The man's voice faded away as he cried out, "Nathaniel! Annabelle!" The receding sound of his heavy footfall blended into the steady wind.

Nathaniel wiped sweat from his forehead with a shaky hand. Was the man gone for good? He felt optimistic for the first time since they had run away. Nathaniel whispered to his sister, who had tucked her head into his midsection, "We have to get to Uncle John's. He'll help us... It's only a little farther."

She grasped his hand.

They crept instinctively through the dark woods. After they had walked a fair distance, Nathaniel recognized a clearing up ahead—the high pasture of his uncle's farm!

He sighed in relief. "We're almost there," he said, hoping to give his sister some reassurance.

Suddenly, Annabelle was yanked from her brother's grip. Then a strong hand grabbed Nathaniel by the back of the neck.

Nathaniel and his sister screamed—woeful, bloodcurdling yelps—as the dull thud of fists on flesh echoed across the pasture.

## CHAPTER 1

# STRANGE DISCOVERY

*Present Day...*

The sweet song of chirping wrens filled the air until interrupted by a siren in the distance, which Tom Sherman heard long before he spotted the patrol car. A little past eight o'clock in the morning, the vehicle turned onto Kingston Club Road.

Tom stood at the entrance to his farm and kicked the metal gate in frustration. In general he respected law officers, but this cop had the hairs on the back of his neck standing on edge. "Why the heck is he blasting that darn siren?" Tom muttered to himself. "So much for keeping this under wraps."

The cruiser pulled just inside the gate, and mercifully the loud noise from the siren stopped. A large man stepped out of the vehicle. Tom walked over to greet the state trooper.

"Are you Mr. Sherman?"

Tom took off his ball cap. He struggled to be polite, still miffed about the siren. "Yes, I am."

"I'm Officer Barton," the trooper said. The two men shook hands. "The dispatcher said you sounded very upset on the phone. What seems to be the problem?"

"I want to show you something that has my nerves on edge." Tom led Officer Barton to his tractor, which he had parked a short distance away. "It's quite a walk to the upper pasture. Hop on."

The officer raised his thick eyebrows and took a step back. "I don't think so… We'll take my cruiser."

"It'll scrape. The road's been washed out for years. My truck has trouble climbing that hill, so your car will never make it. Jump on. It won't take long to get there."

Officer Barton took another look at the old tractor and hesitated. "This thing actually runs?"

Truth be told, the tractor looked more like it belonged in a museum. With its many rust spots, the vehicle appeared multicolored, held together by a mix of parts from several different machines.

Tom lifted his ball cap and scratched his head. He couldn't push the officer onto the tractor; however that's exactly what went through his mind. "She isn't beautiful anymore, but she's reliable," Tom said, as he looked back at the farmhouse. "Just like my wife."

The trooper's face broke out in a wide grin. But he still faced a dilemma—walk or ride? To Tom's relief, the man hopped onto the back of the tractor, immediately grasping the roll bar with his right hand.

Tom started up the old John Deere. White smoke puffed from the exhaust pipe, and the tractor vibrated. When he kicked the machine into gear, the large piece of equipment leaped forward like a horse eager to gallop.

The trooper shouted and grabbed the roll bar with both hands. He squeezed so tightly his knuckles whitened from the pressure.

Tom looked back at the startled officer. "You okay?"

Officer Barton's face had turned ashen, with his lips trembling and nearly colorless. "I…I didn't expect such a kick," he said with a shaky voice.

"Sorry about that. Ol' Nellie is finicky these days. Sometimes she's slow to start, and other times, like today, she can't wait to get going." He patted the hood of the old tractor. "But she always comes through."

Tom stepped on the gas pedal, and soon they traveled up the rugged dirt road. One could easily see the many ruts cut into the narrow lane by numerous heavy rains. Predictably, the tractor ran into a deep furrow, causing it to tip dizzyingly to the right.

The trooper hollered from the back, "Slow down. Whatever's up there isn't going anywhere."

"Oops," Tom said with a slight grin. He figured it was the man's first time on a tractor and had to admit he enjoyed watching the cop's reaction. Nevertheless, anxious to get to the upper pasture, Tom had no intention of slowing down.

"This morning, I noticed my herd acting kind of funny. In fact, a few of them came down from the upper pasture last night. I could tell they were spooked." Tom turned around to face the trooper. "So I rode up the hill to check it out… I couldn't believe what I found."

The trooper's eyes opened wide, and he pointed. "Look out!"

Tom turned back to see a large white oak directly ahead. He had drifted to the left. He cut the wheels sharply to the right and barely missed the massive tree.

Soon after the near crash, the John Deere crested the hill. "It's over there," Tom called out. This time, he looked straight ahead.

An early morning fog bank hugged the ground. Silhouettes of cattle came into view as the two men rode through the pasture. Everything looked peaceful, just what one would expect in rural Derry Township; however, something lay motionless on the ground fifty yards in front of them.

Tom stopped the tractor and turned off the engine. "We'll have to walk from here."

The state trooper leaped off the machine before the large back wheels had come to a complete halt. He ran to an object lying in the field and exclaimed, "What the devil happened?"

CHAPTER 2

# THE ACCIDENT

Matt Monroe rolled over in bed and grabbed for his phone. He rubbed his weary eyes. The screen came into focus, and he pounded his pillow in frustration. How could it be morning already? Matt threw his right arm back in disgust and bumped the headboard. He groaned and pulled the covers over his head.

In recent weeks, Matt had been plagued by strange dreams, night after night awakened by one grisly vision after another. These nightmares exhausted him. Nevertheless, Matt resolved to get his body in motion, for he was the local paperboy, and the *Latrobe Bulletin* came early on Saturdays.

"Bathroom's ready," his brother announced as he walked into the bedroom wrapped in a large towel.

Matt preferred to close his eyes to get a few more minutes of sleep, but nature called. Just the mention of the word *bathroom* made his bladder ache. The Mountain Dew he had drunk before bed begged to be released. He jumped up and nearly bowled Josh over on his way to the toilet.

Josh stood shirtless in front of the large mirror that sat atop the dresser. When Matt entered the bedroom, he noticed the gash on his brother's right side.

Matt winced. "That thing looks infected. It should have healed by now."

"I put some salve on it." Josh stared at him in the mirror. "Don't you say a word to Mom. She'll go ballistic."

It had been almost a month since the injury. His brother's casual attitude confounded Matt. "I think you're taking this way too lightly."

Josh raised his hands. "I'm fine."

The boys finished dressing in silence. Matt looked into the mirror, peering at the awesome amulet he had brought back from Paragon. The ivory mollusk-shaped prize, bestowed on him by Madame Violet of the Elfin High Council, hung around his neck on a gold chain.

Josh whistled.

Matt blushed and quickly tucked the amulet under his T-shirt.

His brother stood in the doorway, snickering.

Matt scrunched his forehead. "What?" he asked, looking in the mirror to make sure his hair wasn't messed up.

"Did you have any crazy dreams last night?" Josh asked.

"No…not last night." Matt stepped into his sneakers. "But I still didn't sleep that well. I'm afraid I'll have another nightmare about Damien."

Josh chuckled. "I don't know about you, Sport, but you attract the weirdest stuff."

"What can I say? It's in the Monroe blood."

After breakfast, Matt sorted his papers and embarked on his Saturday morning paper route. He pedaled past Dr. Steel's house, which sat vacant with a FOR SALE sign posted on the front lawn, amazed how easily the neighbors had bought the story of the old man's death. They were told he'd died of a massive heart attack. To be sure, it was much easier to explain a heart attack than the real reason for Richard Steel's death. His grandson had ordered the body's instant cremation and a small private funeral service held for family only, supposedly according to Dr. Steel's personal wishes. Matt doubted the truthfulness of that story too. To him, it was more a case of expediency over honesty.

Matt turned onto Kingston Club Road. After he placed his last paper in the green plastic paper box in front of the Sherman farm, Matt biked up the hill. As had become his custom since the Paragon incident, he turned left and traveled up the winding lane to the abandoned Victorian mansion that overlooked Kingston.

Crimson maples stood tall on both sides of the driveway. Their branches draped over the roadway. Matt looked up as he rode, admiring the outstretched boughs that created a natural canopy. The trees didn't appear as menacing as that first time he had pedaled up the lane. In fact, now they were a welcome sight—a constant in his life, which had lately turned into a roller coaster.

Thoughts popped into his head of the recent happenings that had occurred on the grounds. The trees had witnessed the entire sequence of events. How many secrets had those trees been privy to in their hundred-plus years of existence? The tales they could tell! Just the actions of the past month alone could fill an entire book and challenge the beliefs of many. Matt's father, Dr. Frank Monroe, told him the truth would only frighten and confuse their neighbors. "What they don't know won't hurt them," his dad had said.

Matt lowered the kickstand and parked his bike near the front porch. He climbed the dilapidated cement steps and looked around as he moseyed onto the wooden porch. The familiar squeaking of loose floorboards announced his arrival.

Connections with this house had changed the direction of his life. Matt thought back to the many bizarre events that had occurred recently. Where to begin? Well, it all started with a mystical ring and set of mysterious wooden tablets, which Matt had found in an old trunk stored in the attic of their farmhouse. Soon after, he and his friends were selected by a secret society to save mankind from an evil elf—pretty wild, huh? They were transported through a portal in the basement of this very house to a world called Paragon, where Josh was attacked by a dragon and got the nasty gash on his right side. And Matt, with the help of his brother and friends, had battled an evil elf, Damien. Ultimately, they were victorious.

Normally one would expect to see bold print headlines in the *Latrobe Bulletin*: **LOCAL TEENS SAVE WORLD**. But since everyone involved was sworn to secrecy, not one of his neighbors knew what Matt and the others had done for them.

He peered into the window and saw a shadow…then…faces, faces in the reflection! Matt jumped back. The window looked forlorn, caked with months of squashed bug parts and grime, long forgotten by its recent owner. He gazed again into the window. This time, Matt saw *his* face staring back at him—no one else. He wiped the sweat from his forehead. *I guess this place will always make me a little jumpy.*

Matt sat on the steps and stared across the front yard. He remembered a time when this property was the pride of Kingston. But those days were long past. Now, gloom oozed from the estate like pus from an infected wound. The grass hadn't been mowed in over a month. It would be taken over by saplings and wild raspberry canes if someone didn't act soon. Agregeous Payne, the owner, was gone, never to return. Matt was sure of that. His father had spread the rumor that the retired dentist moved to Florida to escape the brutal winters of late—another fabrication to shield the good people of Kingston from the naked truth.

After his brief respite, Matt pedaled down Kingston Club Road. His mind wandered, allowing his imagination to travel faster than his bike. Suddenly, a green Chevy pickup truck pulled out directly in front of him. Matt swerved, but the vehicle's right fender clipped his front wheel, and he was thrown off the bicycle onto the pavement.

Tom Sherman quickly yelled from the truck, "Oh my God, are you all right?"

A little dazed, Matt experienced pain from his elbows and knees, which were skinned and bleeding.

He saw his bike lying in the road. The badly bent front wheel wobbled up and down as it spun round and round until it stopped with a sudden screech.

"I didn't see you," the old farmer said as he jumped from the driver's side of the vehicle. He looked around, as if searching for a witness. "Get in the truck. I'll have my wife look at those cuts." After helping Matt into the passenger's seat, Tom Sherman quickly loaded the damaged bicycle onto the bed of his vehicle.

The pickup truck traveled down the gravel road to the farmhouse, kicking up clouds of dust. Matt glimpsed the farmer's elderly wife, Edna, standing on the porch.

Matt got out of the truck. He walked with a limp.

Edna Sherman put her hands to the sides of her face and hurried down the steps toward Matt. "What happened?"

"We had an accident, Mrs. Sherman."

"I've told you before, the name's Edna. Mrs. Sherman was my mother-in-law." She bent down and took a closer look at Matt's bloody knees.

Tom tapped his wife on the shoulder. "I didn't see him pedaling down the hill and hit him with the truck."

Edna gasped. "How could you be so careless!" After a quick glance at Matt's knees, she said, "It doesn't look too bad. Come inside and I'll dress those wounds."

"I'm fine. It just stings," Matt said, stepping away from the farmer's wife.

"You let me be the judge of that, young man." She grabbed Matt by the arm. "Come inside."

He didn't have much choice in the matter, so Matt followed her up the steps.

The large screen door slammed shut as Matt hobbled into the kitchen. It was your typical country kitchen with a large oblong table in the center of the room, surrounded by open-faced cupboards filled with bowls, dishes, and assorted kitchen gadgets.

Pointing to a chair, Edna said, "Sit. I'll be right back."

Matt pulled the wooden chair out from the table and plopped himself down.

Tom Sherman sat in a chair directly opposite Matt. He drummed his fingers absentmindedly on the table. "I don't know where my head was. Ever since the incident this morning, I've been a nervous wreck."

"What incident?"

Edna entered the room with a first aid kit. She gave her husband a stern look. "You keep that to yourself."

"Look, Ma, I can't keep this a secret."

Matt jumped as Edna touched his banged-up knee with tincture of iodine.

She grabbed Matt's leg. "Sit still. Don't be such a baby."

"You sound just like my mother." Matt flinched again as she continued to clean up the wound rather roughly.

Edna taped a bandage over his right knee and then looked up. Staring directly into Matt's eyes, she said, "Have your mother change the dressing tonight...and don't exercise too much for at least twenty-four hours."

"Well, something happened last—"

"Are you deaf, old man?" Edna asked with her distinctive, high-pitched whine.

Tom ignored his wife. "Anyway, something happened last night on the upper pasture." He slapped his right leg. "Instead of talking, why don't I just show you?"

Edna sighed as she finished dressing Matt's wounds. "What did I just tell you? Don't get him involved in this."

Matt's interest was piqued. *What the heck happened that has them so jumpy?*

"Baloney, woman! He's going to find out through the grapevine, so the boy may as well see it for himself."

Edna slammed the lid down on the first aid kit. "No one can tell you anything! I don't know why I put up with you."

Her husband shrugged her off with a grunt.

Edna picked up the phone. "I'm calling Kay to let her know what happened."

Matt jumped up and tried to grab the telephone. "Please don't call my mom, Mrs. Sherman...Edna. She's a worrywart and will get all upset over nothing."

"Nothing? You were hit by a truck, for gosh sake! I don't care what you say. I'm calling your mother." She turned toward her husband. "I'll tell Kay you'll be bringing her son *straight* home." She pointed out the kitchen window. "Don't you dare take him up there!"

Matt got in on the passenger side of the truck. He expected Tom to drive him directly home, but the vehicle turned sharply to the right and stopped in front of the barn.

"Want to see what all the fuss is about?"

Matt looked back at the farmhouse. "Aren't you going to get in trouble with your wife?"

Why did he ask? He saw the mischief in the old man's eyes.

"It'll be a cold day in you-know-where before I start listening to her." The old farmer tapped Matt's left arm and dropped the keys to the tractor in Matt's lap. "You drive."

"Really!"

"Your dad told me you can handle a tractor."

The stinging in his knees forgotten for now, Matt ran to the old John Deere and started her up. Tom jumped onto the back of the tractor. As Matt backed up the large piece of machinery, he spied Edna on the back porch. She stood with her hands on her hips and a scowl on her face.

In no time, the tractor crested the hill and entered the upper pasture. The cattle greeted them with loud moos.

Tom tapped Matt on the back. "It's over there," he yelled.

Matt stopped the tractor. He saw a scene that baffled him; directly ahead lay two livestock carcasses.

Matt's mouth dropped open. "What happened?"

"That's the million-dollar question."

Matt jumped off the tractor and sprinted to one of the dead steers. He bent down to take a closer look.

"Don't touch anything," Tom called out. "The cops are sending a team back with a vet to examine the remains."

The cattle were mutilated, each carcass torn in two. Only the head and front legs, and a portion of the hind legs remained, lying in the field.

"It looks like something bit them in half."

The old farmer placed his right hand on Matt's shoulder. "My thoughts exactly."

"But what do we have in these woods that could do that?" Matt asked, scratching his head.

"Good question." Tom Sherman looked off toward the nearby woods. "What indeed?"

CHAPTER 3

# MYSTERIOUS STRANGER

Kingston sweltered amid abnormally hot and humid weather for early October. Before going to bed, Matt had opened the second-floor window to ventilate their stuffy bedroom, but the nighttime air hung heavy with not one puff of wind.

"Matt."

Startled, Matt awakened and sat up in bed. "What do you want?" he asked. His brother didn't answer. With a quick glance, he found Josh sound asleep.

"Come to me."

*Now that's not my imagination! Should I wake Josh?* Since his brother hadn't been sleeping very well himself these past few weeks, Matt decided to spare him more drama.

"Down here," a male voice hollered.

Matt jumped out of bed and looked out the window into the backyard. He stared, but didn't see anyone. *It's probably just some of the guys in the Brotherhood goofing off.* He decided to sneak outside and surprise them.

Matt quietly descended the stairs into the kitchen. For sure, he didn't want to wake his parents. He crept out of the house. Immediately, he spotted the storage shed lit by an eerie pale-green light shining through its open door. *It has to be Chad. He's such a clown. But this time the joke's going to be on him.*

He slithered to the shed, hidden in the darkened area of the backyard, the corner not illuminated by his neighbor's lamppost. Matt had to hold back a slight giggle.

As he got about halfway, a dense, low-lying fog filtered into the backyard. Soon the mist rose waist-high. Fear replaced fun.

"Matt Monroe."

Matt tried to back up, but he couldn't move, his feet frozen in place. A cold finger of terror ran along his spine.

The voice came from inside the shed. In an instant Matt felt his entire body drawn toward the tiny outbuilding. The force pulled him to within ten feet of the shed. He struggled to get free, but to no avail.

A dark figure emerged and stood in the doorway of the rustic building. The trespasser's eyes burned with a scarlet hue, and his red eyebrows and bushy sideburns appeared to be pasted on his face. He wore a long black overcoat, which Matt found odd for such a warm night.

The figure stepped outside the shed. "I finally get to meet the famous Matt Monroe."

Obviously, this person knew him, but Matt was sure he had never met the man. "What are you doing in our shed?" he asked, spouting the first thing that came to mind. Suddenly, his head ached and his vision blurred, and then slowly, Matt fell to the ground in a crumpled heap.

"Let go of me," a boy's voice called out.

A little girl whimpered, "Please don't hurt me."

Matt lay powerless on the ground, as the man dragged two children out of the shed and marched them into the shadowy woods. Matt rolled over onto his side and blacked out. When he awoke, his shirt, soaked by heavy dew, stuck to his chest. He rubbed his eyes and yawned, then heard footsteps approach.

"What's going on?" his brother asked, as he reached down to help Matt to his feet.

"That's what I'd like to know."

Josh wore a torn T-shirt and shredded boxer shorts, while mud splattered his body up to his waist.

Matt rubbed the side of his head. "What happened to you?"

"I woke up and you were gone."

Matt snickered as he took a good look at Josh's appearance. "You look like you ran through a mud puddle."

"I've looked everywhere for you," Josh said with a hint of anger in his voice, apparently not in a cheerful mood.

"I've been here the whole time," Matt said in his defense.

Josh glared at him. "Then I guess it's my fault I missed you lying in the dark."

*Why are his clothes torn, and where are his shoes?* Matt didn't dare question his brother. His head pounded with the worst headache he had ever experienced. He tried to stand up with Josh's help, but quickly fell back to the grass. "Let me get my bearings."

"What are you doing out here anyway?" Josh asked.

"The shed was open. I came outside to check it out. I thought Chad and some of the guys were up to something." Matt looked around the backyard. "Hey, did you see that strange man with the two kids?"

"What are you talking about?" Josh asked with a smirk, as he helped Matt to his feet.

"You didn't see them?"

With a raised voice, Josh said, "You were sleepwalking. I'm sure whoever you think you saw was a figment of your imagination."

Matt looked at the shed. "If I was dreaming, can you explain why the shed door's wide open?"

"I bet you opened it yourself and just can't remember."

"Someone opened it, I tell you."

"Whatever," Josh said as he locked up the shed. He helped Matt into the kitchen and up the backstairs, careful not to wake their parents.

Once they entered their bedroom and closed the door, Matt said emphatically, "I wasn't dreaming. They were real."

"Face it, they were just characters in another one of your strange dreams."

Matt climbed into bed and said in a low whisper, "I'm telling you for the last time… It wasn't a dream." He pulled the covers over his head.

"Rise and shine, sleepyhead," Josh said in a voice much too cheerful for that early in the morning.

Matt sat up and stretched. "I'm wiped out. I didn't get much sleep." Recollections of what had happened in the backyard flooded his consciousness. "That man was creepy."

Josh sat down on the end of his bed as he stepped into his school shoes. "Maybe it's time we tell Dad about your dreams."

"No way! You know how he is. If you tell him, he'll tell Mom. And that's last thing I need."

Josh grabbed his tie and sports jacket. "I guess you're right. I'll see you downstairs."

## CHAPTER 4

# CHESTNUT MOUNTAIN ACADEMY

The scenic drive to Chestnut Mountain Academy took about ten minutes from Kingston. Matt and his best friend, Zach Roundtree, appreciated the opportunity to ride to school in Josh's classic 1980 Camaro, instead of taking the yellow school bus with all the other freshmen. His brother pulled into his favorite spot in the back of the student parking lot.

Sean O'Leary took the space beside them. Matt identified Sean's car without looking, because of the roaring engine. Sean's vintage Mustang convertible was his trademark.

Josh stepped out, donned his sunglasses, and strutted toward the back of his car. Zach jumped out from the backseat. Matt followed close behind, yawning and rubbing the side of his head. His headache had returned.

Sean, who had traveled to Paragon with Matt and Josh, gathered books from the trunk of his car, tossing them into an open backpack. He turned around, took a long look at Matt, and raised his eyebrows. "You look terrible."

"I didn't sleep too well last night," Matt said with a big yawn.

Sean peered over toward Josh. "Whew, you look worse than your brother."

"That cut from the dragon... I think it's infected. It's really wiping me out," Josh said.

"What did the doctor say?"

Josh slipped his backpack over his shoulder. "Haven't seen one."

"You've got to be kidding me. You have no idea what kind of germs that thing could've been carrying."

Josh walked over to Sean and patted him on the cheek. "Okay, Mommy. I'll be a good boy and get it checked out today."

Sean hit Josh's hand away. He looked over to Matt, as if for help.

"What?" Matt asked, wondering what Sean thought he could do about the situation. "I agree with you. I think he should get it checked."

Sean looked back at Josh. "I know you think you're invincible, but you're nuts if you don't get it looked at."

"Just chill. I've been putting antibacterial salve on it... It's getting better."

Sean threw another book into his backpack. "Whatever, it's your funeral."

By this time, Matt's head throbbed. "What's taking you so long?" he asked. Tired of waiting, he walked over to the car and looked into the trunk. It was littered with books and piles of papers, along with various pieces of sports equipment. "Man, you are such a slob."

Sean gave Matt an odd look. "What? You don't like my filing system?" He slammed the top of the trunk down with a forceful shove. "Let's roll."

As they approached the front entrance of the school, Zach whispered to Matt, "It looks like everyone's waiting for Josh and Sean. It's so cool to be with them."

Matt placed his arm on his friend's shoulder. "Yeah, but never let Josh hear you say that. His head's big enough already. Just about every girl swoons if he even smiles at them."

Before he stepped across the roadway, Matt stopped and stared at the main building on campus. Franklin Hall, an impressive, enduring structure built over a hundred years earlier, was a large three-story edifice, encased in brown limestone. Over the years, many buildings had been added to the campus, with Pear Memorial Library being the latest. But Franklin Hall far outshone the others. Its stately appearance reflected the credentials of its faculty and the high standards of education exemplified by the school.

"Hi, guys," Katie O'Hara called from the front steps of Franklin Hall. Matt and Katie had known each other since kindergarten. She ran up to them. "You're late. Even the bus beat you here."

Josh pointed to Matt. "That's because my little brother couldn't get his butt out of bed this morning."

Matt sneered, even though his brother was spot-on in his appraisal of the situation.

Josh walked up and put his arm around Katie's waist. He gave her a peck on the cheek. "How's our little princess this morning?"

Katie blushed. She obviously loved the attention. But what happened to the girl Matt used to know? Paragon had changed her, that's for sure. Katie had her hair styled and actually wore a gray skirt instead of her standard gray slacks.

Three attractive cheerleaders—school royalty, all of them—stood near the main entrance: Mitzi Martel, Brittany Benton, and Dani Halverson.

Matt and Zach quickly ducked past the three girls with no incident.

"This place couldn't exist without the three witches," Zach whispered sarcastically to Matt.

Matt burst into laughter. He turned around and caught an evil look from Mitzi.

Josh hustled past the cheerleaders with Katie in tow.

"Morning, Josh," the girls said in unison.

Mitzi stepped forward. "Josh, I hope you're planning to come to the Halloween dance. It's going to be special this year…*real* special. You'll never guess where we plan to hold it."

Josh muttered, "Whatever, I'm sure it'll be nice." He purposely put his arm around Katie, steering her away from the three girls.

Matt loved the way his brother handled the divas. The girls appeared to have everything, but there was one thing, or more precisely, one boy they didn't have—Josh Monroe.

Mitzi and Brittany glowered with pursed lips and reddened cheeks, but the appearance of genuine hurt filled Dani's eyes. The cheerleaders stomped away.

Sean grabbed Josh roughly. "That was kind of rude, don't you think?"

Josh pushed his hand away. "You want to hang with them, be my guest," he said loudly. "They're in love with themselves."

"Yeah, I agree Brittany and Mitzi are stuck-up, but Dani's all right."

Josh grumbled. "That's your opinion."

"Katie, Katie!" The high-pitched voice of Sydney Mason, one of the few girls Katie associated with, broke up the heated conversation. "Did you finish your essay?"

Katie tapped her backpack. "Yep, it was actually fun."

Zach snickered. "You are such a geek!"

"Like you're not," Katie said mockingly. "Just because you get to hang with the coolest guys in school doesn't make you one of them." Bam! Score one for Katie.

Zach headed down the hall alone. Either Katie didn't realize how hurtful her comment had been, or she didn't care.

Katie scurried away with her girlfriend. "See you first period," she hollered back to Matt.

Matt couldn't believe how insensitive Katie had gotten. He didn't answer and dashed to catch up with Zach. "Ignore her. She can be a jerk sometimes."

Zach shrugged. "I don't care what she says. It doesn't bother me." His eyes betrayed him, but Matt decided not to push the issue.

Their lockers stood next to each other. Matt opened his locker door and quickly searched for his bottle of aspirin. He discreetly swallowed two pills with a quick swig of bottled water.

"I met the new history teacher, the dude who's filling in for Mrs. Bishop," Zach said, reaching for a textbook on the top shelf of his locker. "We were having dinner at Dino's on Saturday, and he came over to our table. Turns out he knew my dad at Pitt."

Matt figured it was an attempt to change the subject, so he played along. "What was he like?"

"In a word…intimidating."

Matt scrunched his forehead. "Intimidating…how?"

"First off, his name is Hardcastle…Mr. Oliver Hardcastle."

"Ooh, he sounds sophisticated."

"Not sure about that, but he has a deep voice and talks real fast, like he's nervous or something."

Matt leaned against his locker. "Oh great! It'll be tough taking notes in his class."

"He looks ex-military," Zach said, as he stuffed two textbooks into his backpack. "I don't think he'll take any guff from anyone."

A familiar voice, from across the hall, interrupted their conversation. "Good morning, gentlemen."

Matt looked up and saw Dr. Herman Grant, the school psychologist. "Good morning, sir."

"Did you have a good weekend?" Both boys nodded. "I hope you enjoyed my Friday lecture."

"It was the best, Dr. Grant," Matt blurted out. He blushed when he realized how that must have sounded.

The counselor smiled, evidently pleased with the response. "Very well then, I'll see you later."

"Sure thing, Dr. Grant," Zach said, snickering.

Matt looked down to the floor. "He probably thinks I'm a dope."

"No…more like a suck-up."

Matt moaned. "That's even worse."

"But you're right. His lectures are always fun."

Out of nowhere, a blunt force hit Matt. He bounced off the front of his locker.

Rico Steel stood close by with a smug expression on his face. Rico, well known as the school bully, picked on anyone as long as his target was younger and smaller. A senior, he stood over six feet tall with a muscular build, while Matt, a lowly freshman, stood five foot, eight inches tall with a thin build. Enough said.

In an instant, Brian McGuire, a friend of the Monroe brothers, grabbed Rico and slammed him into a nearby locker, holding the bully against the metal door with both hands. Brian gritted his teeth and said firmly, "If you *ever* touch that kid again, I'll flatten you. I'll never understand why he saved your sorry butt in Paragon."

Suddenly, a tall, muscular stranger pulled the boys apart. He had no trouble handling the two students, who looked like helpless rabbits caught in the grasp of a hawk's talons. There was no escape. The man walked down the hall with Rico and Brian, one in each arm. Dr. Grant followed hastily after them.

Zach poked Matt. "That's Mr. Hardcastle."

Matt stared until the man turned left and disappeared with Brian and Rico. "Wow! He does look ex-military. I wouldn't want to get on his bad side."

A loud, excited voice carried up the hall. Chad McGuire stood in front of the gym, flailing his arms. Even though Matt couldn't quite make out the gist of the conversation, Sean, Josh, and other senior members of the swim team were listening intently to what Chad had to say.

The older boys headed out a side door that led to the sports fields. Matt and Zach decided to follow them.

"What happened?" Matt asked, sprinting to catch up with the others.

Chad glared. "Someone turfed the soccer field and smashed some of the benches."

"What?" Zach asked. "Who would do something that stupid?"

Josh looked over. "Who do you think? A total loser...and we all know who that is."

"Rico?" Matt asked.

Sean nodded. "He has to be involved somehow."

The school bell rang, which meant they had ten minutes to get to their first-period class. "We'd better go back. I don't want to be late for biochem," Josh said.

"We can check it out at lunch," Chad said, as the boys hurried toward Franklin Hall.

After they entered the building, Matt noticed Brian walking toward them. His friend had a scowl on his face.

Chad stopped his brother. "Hey, what's up? You look like you lost your best friend."

"Three-day suspension for fighting," Brian said disgustedly.

"What?" Chad looked confused.

"Rico hit Matt against his locker this morning," Brian said. "I retaliated. So I got suspended."

"Well, at least Rico got three days out," Matt said, in relief.

"Nope," Brian said tersely. "The new teacher, Mr. Hardcastle, said it was *my* fault. He said he was in the back hall the whole time and never saw Rico hit you. Can you believe that? Dr. Grant tried to step in, but old lady Watson wouldn't listen."

Matt clenched his teeth.

Brian punched a locker. "Hardcastle told her I was a liar. She believed him, so now I'm suspended and Rico got nothing, not even a warning."

Matt couldn't believe it. "That's not right. I'm going to the office to straighten this out."

Brian grabbed Matt's arm. "Don't waste your time. Since Hardcastle said Rico didn't hit you, they'll just think you made it up to help me...and you'll get suspended for lying."

Chad dug into his pants and pulled out a set of car keys. He tossed them to his brother. "Drive my car home. I'll catch a ride with Sean. Don't worry... I'll get Rico."

Brian jumped up and grabbed a low-hanging banner advertising the Halloween dance. With one pull, the sign lay in ruins on the floor of the back hall. "This place sucks."

Chad slammed a fist into his left hand. "Rico's dead meat," he muttered.

"Don't go there, Chad." The new voice took the boys by surprise. It was Dr. Grant. Where had he come from?

Chad jumped when he heard the counselor. "Sorry, sir. I didn't see you standing there."

"Well, it's good I overheard you. One more incident and you'll be on probation."

Tired of the injustice, Matt blurted out, "But Brian's innocent. Rico *did* shove me into my locker."

"I know. I was there, remember?"

Matt stomped his foot. "But Dr. Grant, then you know Brian wasn't lying."

"Whether Rico started it or not doesn't matter. Brian retaliated... That's the point."

Matt watched the look of a wild man emerge in Chad's eyes.

"That's crap, and you know it," Chad said, his lower jaw quivering.

Dr. Grant placed his hands firmly on Chad's shoulders, holding him in place. "Let me explain something to you, young man. I did see Rico push Matt into the locker... But it wasn't Brian's place to settle the score. You understand me?"

This didn't calm Chad down one bit. In fact, it riled him all the more. He tried to pull free from the teacher's grasp.

Dr. Grant squeezed Chad's shoulders a little tighter. "One more fight and you could be expelled. I'd hate to see that happen over a troublemaker like Rico Steel." With that said, the teacher strolled down the hall.

Josh punched Chad lightly in the arm. "You'd better cool it. You're going to get screwed if you try to deal with Rico on your own. Forget him. He's not worth the trouble."

Chad grimaced. "That's easy for you to say. But if I see him out of school, he's going to be one sorry sucker."

The boys separated and headed to their respective classes.

CHAPTER 5

# FOOTPRINTS IN TIME

Matt raced to the third-floor classroom, and the bell rang just as he stepped over the threshold. He gave a short fist pump because he had beaten the bell…barely. You see, Mr. Robert Werner was not a tolerant man, especially when it came to tardiness. On the first day of school, he had told the class, "Tardiness shows a complete lack of planning, and it's a sure sign one is destined for failure."

Matt rushed over to his seat near the window and quickly sat down. He breathed heavily from his quick climb up two flights of stairs. Matt looked over and spotted Katie, who rolled her eyes.

The first nine-week grading period was devoted to Shakespeare's *Romeo and Juliet*. Matt sighed deeply for he found his first-period class, English Literature, boring at best. He could not see the relevance of medieval writing in modern times. He hadn't gotten a good night's sleep in over two weeks, so it took no time for Mr. Werner's calm, steady voice to lull Matt into a dream state.

"Mr. Monroe."

Matt jumped to attention, startled by the sound of his name. "Yes, sir?"

"Can you tell me what Mr. Shakespeare meant to convey in this passage?"

Matt gulped. He had no idea which part of the play Mr. Werner referred to. "Well…I feel…um—"

"Spare us your lack of preparation." Mr. Werner's slow, methodical tone left no room for discussion. "But I warn you, daydream in my class again, and I will make your life interesting, to say the least."

"Sorry, sir. It won't happen again."

The stuffy room sweltered, and the open windows gave no relief from the excessive heat and humidity. As the teacher droned on and on, Matt tried his best to remain attentive, but no matter how hard he tried to listen, he found himself daydreaming again. Matt gazed out the window. From this vantage point, he saw the soccer field.

As he stared at the field, he had a revelation. Matt jumped up and ran to the window. "The field wasn't turfed!" he exclaimed.

Mr. Werner stopped his lecture. Silence fell over the room. It was so quiet one could hear the train running through the far side of town.

Matt rushed back to his seat.

Mr. Werner slammed his textbook closed. "Enlighten us, Mr. Monroe. Please."

Matt experienced blood rushing to his face. He peered at Katie, who sat on the other side of the room. For some crazy reason he thought she could help him.

Mr. Werner walked halfway down the aisle. "Maybe you have a hearing problem too, young man. Please enlighten us. What caused your outburst in *my* class?"

"Sorry, sir. It won't happen again."

"This seems to be your mantra," the teacher said. He repeated in a high-pitched, mocking voice, "Sorry, sir. It won't happen again."

The class broke out in spontaneous laughter.

Mr. Werner marched to Matt's desk and thumped his copy of *Romeo and Juliet* down on the flat wooden surface. The sound reverberated around the room. The snickering stopped. "Mr. Shakespeare may have approved of your dramatics, but I can assure you I do not. Do I make myself perfectly clear?"

Matt wanted to crawl inside his desk and hide. "Yes, sir. Perfectly clear."

The bell rang, signaling the end of class. Matt looked up, somewhat relieved, only to find himself staring directly into Mr. Werner's dark brown eyes. Matt gave a sheepish grin.

"Make sure you get a good night's sleep, Mr. Monroe. I *will* be calling on you tomorrow." The teacher walked away and then pivoted to face Matt. "And I expect to get an intelligent answer, not 'Um... well' or 'I feel...'" Mr. Werner winked before he turned away and left the room.

Matt breathed a long sigh of relief.

Katie ran over to Matt. "What were you thinking?"

Feeling a little more settled, he stood and walked to the window. "Quick, look out the window. What do you see?" He pointed to the soccer field.

Katie followed his finger. "The turfed field and the smashed benches? *Everyone* knows about that. It's old news."

"The field wasn't turfed. Those aren't tire tracks," Matt said excitedly. "They're footprints."

"What! You and your imagination... Get a life."

Undeterred by her response, Matt calmly said, "Take another look."

Katie huffed a bit, but turned around and stared at the soccer field.

"You don't see the footprints?" Matt asked.

"Are you kidding me?" Katie sauntered away, chuckling.

Matt scrunched his forehead, stunned by her response. He leaned against the windowsill. "They *are* footprints," he said to himself. "Why can't she see that?"

## CHAPTER 6

# MR. HARDCASTLE

At lunch, Matt explained his footprints theory in detail to Zach and Katie. Zach, responsive at first, ended up agreeing with Katie that the ruts in the field were caused by car or truck tires. Upset, Matt sat back in his chair and crossed his arms. *Why won't anybody believe me? This day can't get any worse.* Then Matt remembered... Mr. Oliver Hardcastle taught his next class, Early American History. He gulped loudly.

Matt peered into the second-floor classroom. "He's not here," he said to Zach, who stood nearby. Matt waved Zach forward. "You've got to see this."

Zach looked into the room. "That's interesting!"

The desks, arranged in a semicircle, had student's names taped on top of them. Matt quickly found his desk, then glanced from side to side. To his left sat John Black, a kid he had known since fourth grade. *That's cool*, he thought. But on his right, clearly marked in bold black lettering, Matt spotted the name—Rico Steel. He muttered, "Just great."

Students filtered in, and just as the bell rang to start class, Rico Steel stumbled into the room. He quickly took his seat and made sure to bump into Matt's desk, knocking his textbook onto the floor. As Matt leaned over to pick up the book, Rico snickered. "Oops."

Matt grabbed his history book and glared at the bully. Before he could say anything, Mr. Hardcastle walked into the room. The class quickly stood at attention.

"Sit," he commanded. "My name is Mr. Hardcastle. I am filling in for Mrs. Bishop for the foreseeable future. I looked over your individual records and see that we are blessed with a senior student in this class. I'm sure he will be able to share his wealth of knowledge on the subject."

Matt chuckled.

"What's so funny, geek?" Rico asked in a whisper. His eyes narrowed in contempt.

Matt loved it. Mr. Hardcastle must have reconsidered his first impression of Rico. Why was a senior sitting in a freshman history class, anyway? Matt hoped Rico would get the bulk of the teacher's grief.

Mr. Hardcastle leaned against his desk. "Early American History is a study of events that changed the world. Our discussions will center on a group of men who had the courage of their convictions to break away from the most powerful country on earth in order to form a constitutional democracy." He looked across the room. "Can anyone tell me something about our founding fathers?"

Silence; everyone sat motionless, looking down at their desks. This subject was old news to all of them. Rehashing it was not exactly something Matt relished. He glanced at Zach, who raised his eyebrows; obviously, his friend felt the same.

"Mr. Roundtree. What can you tell me about John Adams?"

Zach stared straight ahead, totally still, as though frozen.

"Mr. Roundtree, I'm waiting."

Not very comfortable speaking in front of a group, Zach stood. His right leg twitched slightly. He mumbled, "John Adams is most known for—"

"Louder, Mr. Roundtree," the teacher said scornfully. "I'm sure everyone would love to hear your words of wisdom."

Zach gasped audibly, and the class broke into light laughter.

Rico yelled out, "Better watch yourself, or Fat Boy will start to cry."

Matt wanted to punch Rico in the mouth.

"One more outburst, Mr. Steel, and you'll spend the rest of this period in the office," Mr. Hardcastle said curtly. "Do I make myself clear?"

As soon as the teacher had turned his attention back to Zach, Matt whispered to Rico, "What do you think about that, dummy?"

Rico punched Matt in the arm, nearly knocking him out of his seat.

"Ow!" Matt yelped.

Mr. Hardcastle turned toward Matt. A look of disdain spread across the man's face. "That will be enough of that."

"He punched me," Matt said, rubbing his arm. "Didn't you see it?"

The teacher marched over to Matt's desk, stomping on the hardwood floorboards with each step. "How dare you give me that tone of voice!" Mr. Hardcastle peered at Matt's name tag on the desk. He paused, and his eyes widened. "Wait a minute; you're the boy from this morning's incident."

"And you're the man who's selective in what he sees." *Did I actually say that?* Matt wasn't sure where he'd summoned the courage—or the stupidity—to utter the comment out loud. He glanced over at Zach, who stood with a look of terror in his eyes.

The teacher's face turned red. "What did you say?"

Matt stood up, his eyes filled with rage; his anger over Brian's suspension was at a boiling point. "You said Rico didn't ram me into my locker this morning, but he did, and you know he did. And Rico punched me just now. Just ask anyone in this room, and they'll tell you!"

"That's enough. Get out of my class and report to Mrs. Watson."

Matt scowled at the teacher. "Gladly!" He grabbed his backpack and bolted out of the room.

Matt stood alone in the hall and freaked out. *What did I do? I've never talked back to a teacher before.* Mr. Hardcastle had pushed all the right buttons. *What kind of teacher lies to the headmistress? What kind of teacher picks on a student?*

He descended the stairs. With each step, his fury intensified...until he saw the main office. The well-lit room, designed with glass walls, lay directly ahead. Quickly, Matt's anger turned into regret, and then fear.

The office secretary, Mrs. Parker, sat at her desk, typing away at her keyboard. A close friend of the Monroe family, she looked up when Matt entered the office and greeted him warmly. "Hi, Matt. What can I do for you?"

Matt blushed with embarrassment. He had never been sent to the office before, at least not for discipline. He mumbled, "Mr. Hardcastle sent me."

"What does he need?" she asked, obviously unaware of Matt's predicament.

Matt panicked; he felt warm. He looked up and saw a concerned look on the woman's face.

"Are you all right?" Mrs. Parker asked.

Matt sweated profusely; the room started to spin, and suddenly everything went black.

Matt woke up and looked around. When Dr. Amil Habib entered the curtained cubicle, Matt instantly knew where he was—Latrobe Hospital's emergency room. He had been there many times before when his illness had flared up. Just the thought nauseated him.

Quick thinking by the attending nurse saved the day. She placed a silver basin to his mouth just as he let go. Vomit splashed into the container.

Matt spied his mother through the partially opened curtain. That didn't surprise him, but when he noticed his dad standing beside her, it confirmed his fears; his illness had returned!

Dr. Habib stared at the monitor connected to Matt. Matt's heart rate and blood pressure had climbed. "What's going on, buddy?"

In mere seconds, his parents sat by his bed. Dr. Habib was no longer there.

"You gave us a scare," his father said.

His mother walked over and offered him some ice water. Matt took a quick sip. "What happened?" he asked.

"You collapsed in the school office," she said. "But your blood work came back normal." He could hear relief in her voice.

"Dad, if I'm not sick, what happened to me?"

His father leaned over the bed and grabbed Matt's right hand. "Dr. Habib thinks you had a panic attack."

"A panic attack!" Matt sat up in bed, his face flushed; he was mortified because he figured only girls had panic attacks.

His dad laughed. "You know, there are easier ways to get out of class."

Matt loved his father's sense of humor. He picked up a small pillow and tossed it in his dad's direction. The cushion sailed past its target.

At precisely that moment, Dr. Habib walked back into the cubicle. He dodged the pillow with surprising agility as it zipped through the opened curtain. "Looks like somebody's ready to go home," the doctor said with a big grin.

"Are you sure?"

Matt could see things were back to normal for his mother, the worrywart.

Dr. Habib closed the metal chart. "Yes. In fact, he can be discharged as soon as you sign the papers."

"Thanks, Amil." Matt's dad shook the doctor's hand. "Kay, let's give Matty his privacy."

She looked at Dr. Habib. "You're sure he's okay?"

"Yes, Kay. He's fine. But I do think it would be wise to keep him out of school for a few days."

Matt's mom remained in the cubicle until the nurse unhooked his IV and monitor. "We'll be just outside in the hall when you're ready," she said.

"I thought she'd never leave," Matt said, looking for his clothes.

The doctor pointed to a side cupboard. "In there." Dr. Habib studied Matt's chart. "You definitely had a panic attack. I want to arrange some counseling sessions with the school psychologist."

Matt breathed a sigh of relief. "I know Dr. Grant. Yeah, I guess that'd be all right."

"I'm glad you approve," Dr. Habib said with a hint of a smile. "I'll check with your father and have him set up an appointment."

# CHAPTER 7
# THE GRUDGE

The red sportscar roared into the driveway, barely missing the lonely mailbox with the name **STEEL** stenciled on its side. Heavy metal blasted from the stereo as the sleek automobile sped down the long driveway toward a secluded brick house. Massive white pine trees camouflaged the sprawling ranch so well one had to stare to see the outline of the residence.

Rico hit the brakes hard and parked his convertible in front of the two-car garage. He grabbed his backpack and raced to the kitchen. Rico tossed his car keys on the kitchen counter.

"Is that you, Rico?" a voice hollered from deep within the house.

"Yeah, Dad."

"I want to talk with you," his father shouted.

Rico figured his dad had heard about the skirmish with Matt at school. He strutted into the study and was pleased to see a big grin on his father's face.

"Well done, Son. I got the call from school," his dad said, raising a glass of scotch in a symbolic toast. "Just be careful not to push things too far too fast, or you could get suspended."

Rico sat in front of the ornate desk that dominated the room. He picked up a photo and stared at the image of his mother and himself on their last family vacation in Disney World. Tears filled his eyes. Rico was only twelve years old when a coal truck crossed the center line on Route 711 and hit his mother's car head-on. She died instantly. He and his mom had been very close, and her sudden death had affected him deeply.

His father said gently, "I miss her too."

Rico placed the photo back on his father's desk. "Dad, I have something to say. Please don't get mad."

"What is it?"

Rico dreaded this moment because his father wouldn't like what he had to say. "I think picking on Matt is wrong," he mumbled, ready for a verbal explosion.

His father slammed his drink down on the desk, splattering the oak surface with droplets of the strong liquor. "What? Your great-grandfather is dead because of that kid!"

Rico looked up. His lips quivered as he spoke softly. "Pap caused his own death. He's the one who messed up in Paragon."

"How can you say that?" His father lunged across the desk and grabbed Rico's left shoulder. "He tried to help you, to make you the hero in Paragon. But that damn family interfered and caused his death." He released Rico and leaned back in his comfy chair.

Rico dared not move, stunned by his dad's aggression. He recognized the misery in his father's tired eyes. "Dad, I agree with you. The Monroes are stuck-up jerks. But it looks bad for me when I pick on a younger kid. Matt has lots of friends. Every one of the guys in the Brotherhood defends him. Brian McGuire saw me slam him into the locker. He would have pounded me if the new teacher hadn't stopped him. Just about everyone in school hates me."

Anger flashed across his father's face. "Those McGuires are just about as much trouble as the Monroes. But didn't I raise you better? Isn't it obvious?"

"What do you mean?" Rico asked, leaning forward.

His father took another sip of his drink. "Since you don't want to get Matt personally, divide and conquer. Get them to fight among themselves."

Rico leaned back in the chair and placed both hands behind his head, cradling his neck. "How do I do that?"

His father stood up quickly. "Do I have to think of everything? Find a way to get them at each other's throats. I don't know. Spread rumors… Get a girl between them."

Rico smiled broadly and pounded the desk. "I know exactly what I can do. I don't know why I didn't think of it before."

"Now that's my boy!"

The Monroe brothers had to pay.

CHAPTER 8

# HEADMISTRESS

"Why are you dressed for school?"

"Mom, I'm fine." Matt reached for the cereal box. "I'm going crazy sitting here at home. I want to go to school."

"That's simply out of the question," Kay Monroe said firmly.

Josh winked at Matt. "Mom, it's Friday. If he goes to school today, he'll have two days to recuperate over the weekend. And if he gets panicky, I can always drive him home."

Matt flashed a sly grin, for they had practiced this very dialogue in their bedroom that morning.

His mom leaned against the sink. "That does make sense." She looked at her husband. "What do you think?"

Frank Monroe lowered the morning paper. "I think the boys are right. Matty looks ready to get back in the swing of things."

She hesitated for a moment, then agreed. "Okay, let's give it a try. But if you start to feel the least bit upset, you call me."

Matt and Josh gave each other a low five under the table.

Matt spotted Katie, Zach, and a few other friends standing near the entrance to Franklin Hall.

Katie hugged Matt. "Are you okay? You had us worried."

Zach gave him a fist bump. "We heard the ambulance siren. When it pulled up to the school, everyone freaked out. But we had no clue it was for you."

Matt shrugged. "I have no idea what happened." Of course, he wasn't going to tell them about his panic attack.

"When we found out you collapsed, I lost it." Katie gave Matt another hug. "Please don't scare me like that again!"

"Sorry to cause such a scene."

Katie punched Matt lightly on the shoulder. "Why didn't you answer any of my texts?"

"My mom took my phone. She told me I needed to rest. It about drove me nuts." Matt automatically patted his pocket, reaching for his phone. "Crap, she still has it!"

"Josh wasn't much help either," Zach said. "All he said was that you were okay."

They walked into the school, and other students went out of their way to greet Matt.

Out of the corner of his eye, Matt spied Mr. Hardcastle. Ducking his head, he whispered to Zach, "Look who's standing over there. Just who I wanted to see first thing this morning."

Matt smiled sheepishly as he passed the stern teacher; he half expected Mr. Hardcastle to march him directly to the headmistress's office.

"Mr. Monroe," the teacher said tersely.

Matt gulped. He was sure Mr. Hardcastle heard his loud swallow.

"You got away this time, but don't rely on health issues to get out of your next predicament. Don't cross me again."

Zach stuck his tongue out and made an obnoxious noise as the teacher walked away.

Matt snickered, knowing full well his friend would have collapsed had Mr. Hardcastle turned back.

"Well, you guys said he was a jerk," Katie said. "Nailed it."

Just then, the headmistress stepped into the hall. She waved at the three freshmen students. "Matthew Monroe, come here." She motioned him forward with a crooked index finger.

Matt muttered to his friends, "Maybe I didn't get away with anything after all."

Mrs. Evelyn Watson had been on staff at the academy for over forty years, serving the past ten years as headmistress. Meticulous in her appearance, with not a hair out of place and her makeup barely visible, she was a taller and thinner version of Leota Witherspoon, the recently retired librarian.

The headmistress had the final say in all matters at the school. Matt took a deep breath. *This can't be good.*

Once they entered her private office, Mrs. Watson offered Matt a seat. They were separated by a large antique oak desk. Framed photographs filled the right side of her desk—family, no doubt. The room wasn't anywhere near as luxurious as he had imagined it.

Matt worried how this little meeting would unfold. He had heard she was fair in her dealings with students, but then there was the Brian incident. Plus, he had talked back to a teacher, which was not taken lightly at the academy.

"Would you like some water?" she asked.

Matt jumped when he heard her voice; he had been lost in his thoughts, imagining the many awful punishments he could receive. "Oh, no thank you. I'm fine." He fidgeted in the solid oak chair, causing a low-pitched squeak.

Mrs. Watson leaned back. "Relax, Matthew. You're not on trial here. I just wanted to see how you were feeling. Your father told me about your medical condition before term started. We on the staff have been watching you closely."

Matt grumbled, and the headmistress chuckled. His groan was obviously louder than he had intended.

"I was glad to hear it was nothing serious," she said, with a tone of sincere empathy.

Mrs. Watson was not going to punish him. Relieved, he said, "Thanks."

"So how are you enjoying high school so far?"

Matt shrugged.

"It's always tough when you're taken out of your comfort zone." Mrs. Watson stood and walked around the desk, which Matt took as his cue to rise. "I expect great things from you. Your entrance exam scores were exceptional. But then again, I wouldn't expect anything less from a son of Frank Monroe."

Matt felt relaxed enough to ask her about the recent vandalism. "So any news on who damaged the soccer field?"

She appeared taken aback by the question and fumbled for an answer. "No…no, not really. But we're keeping our eyes and ears open."

Matt walked to the door. He turned the doorknob, but before he opened the oak door, he said, "You know everyone seems to think the field was turfed by a truck or something."

"Yes, that's the general consensus."

Matt let go of the doorknob and turned back to face Mrs. Watson. With excitement in his voice, he said, "The field wasn't turfed. Some kind of animal did it."

The headmistress gave Matt a most peculiar look. "I never thought of that possibility," she said without any sign of ridicule. "I guess it's something I'll have to consider then, won't I?"

"You'll see I'm right."

Mrs. Watson escorted Matt out of her office. As they stepped into the hall, she leaned close to him. "We'll solve the mystery of the turfed field. But I would advise you to control your temper when talking with a teacher—especially Mr. Hardcastle. He has zero tolerance for disobedience, even when a certain bully is more at fault for starting the incident."

There it was. She knew the truth but had let him off the hook this time. He was sure that was why Mr. Hardcastle had been so gruff that morning. "Yes, ma'am."

The headmistress touched his shoulder quite gently. "Rico Steel's not worth a suspension, is he?"

"No, ma'am," he said meekly. And with that, Matt raced down the hall. He couldn't get out of there fast enough. He quickly turned the corner and ran directly into Dr. Grant.

"Sorry, sir. I should have—"

Dr. Grant held Matt by his shoulders. "No problem. You're just the boy I've been looking for."

Matt furrowed his brow. "You're looking for me?"

"Your dad wants me to meet twice a week with you." The counselor lowered his voice. "It's about your panic attack. I suggest we use part of your lunch period. I've cleared my schedule and penciled you in at that time. Let's say Mondays and Wednesdays. Is that good for you?"

*I only agreed to the sessions to get Mom off my back.* "Sure… I guess. I'll see you then," he said with uncertainty.

Dr. Grant searched Matt's concerned face. "I'm a professional. Everything you tell me is in confidence. No one, not even your parents, will hear a word of what we discuss."

Matt smiled faintly as he walked away from Dr. Grant. There was no way he could renege on the sessions. *At least it's Dr. Grant who'll be counseling me. What if Mr. Hardcastle were the school psychologist?* The thought horrified him.

Zach waited for Matt at their lockers. It didn't take long for the inquisition to begin. "What did Mrs. Watson want?"

Matt attempted to play down the meeting. "Oh, she just wanted to know how I was feeling."

"So she didn't punish you for telling off Hardcastle?"

"No, she was really nice… I told her my theory about the damage to the soccer field," Matt said, trying to steer the conversation away from the Hardcastle incident.

"And?" Zach asked with a large grin and a slight chuckle.

"She was polite and didn't laugh. But I'm not so sure she took me seriously."

Zach closed his locker door. "Well, you have to admit it does seem a little farfetched. If they were footprints, that animal would be gigantic."

"I see you're back, wimp!"

Matt didn't have to turn around. He knew that voice—Rico Steel. Oddly, when the troublemaker passed the two boys, he didn't push them. He didn't move a bit in their direction. Matt peered down the hall and saw why. Chad stood near the gym entrance. Matt gave him a thumbs-up.

Zach tapped Matt on the shoulder. "Rico's not so brave when Chad's around."

## CHAPTER 9

# THE BREAK-IN

The abandoned campus of Chestnut Mountain Academy sat quiet and peaceful that night after a full day of student activity. The stars shined brightly, and the peal from the bell of the Methodist church traveled unimpeded across town, announcing the time—two in the morning.

Meanwhile, a hooded figure stood at the side entrance of Pear Memorial Library. The intruder looked back and forth, then quickly stepped up to the door and jiggled the lock with some sort of device. After a few twists and turns, the lock clicked. A solid pull with gloved hands opened the large metal door.

The only illumination in the vacant library came from a dim emergency light located on the ceiling in the back hall. Aided by a small flashlight, the trespasser descended into the basement. Using the same device, it didn't take the intruder long to open the lock on the middle cabinet in the stack of books along the far wall. The flashlight lit up the priceless manuscripts, while the burglar's gloved hand grabbed one of the treasures.

Mr. Jasper Green, the sixty-five-year-old night watchman, drove his electric golf cart across the campus every night at regular intervals. There had never been any damage on his watch until the soccer field incident a week earlier. He took the attack personally; it blemished his perfect record. *I should have retired when I had the chance. Kids today have no respect for anything.* He could have sworn one of the boarders had damaged the field, although the security cameras at the dorm hadn't revealed any students leaving the living quarters that night.

The electric cart made its way past Franklin Hall and turned left to circle the library. Jasper moaned and groaned the entire trip. *I don't know what Watson thinks I can do by myself. We need at least one more guard.*

He noticed someone standing at the side entrance of the library. Jasper stopped the cart and turned off the electric engine. He watched as the door opened. The loud squeal of metal echoed across the parking lot, and the intruder hastily entered the building. Jasper pulled the nightstick from his belt and slowly crept toward the door.

The old watchman surveyed the situation. The lock had been tampered with, which meant the delinquent didn't have a key. He carefully opened the door and looked down the hall. He could see nothing until a flicker of light shone up from the basement.

Jasper sneaked down the stairwell. When he reached the bottom of the stairs, he flipped the light switch. With a simple flick, the room lit up bright as a Christmas tree during the holidays.

"I know you're down here." Jasper called. "Come out now. There's no way out of this room."

The old watchman saw what appeared to be a shadow of the prowler slip down the far aisle. "Got you now," he muttered under his breath. He held his nightstick out in front of him with an unsteady right hand, which caused the club to waver slightly.

Jasper walked to the end of the aisle and leaned against the bookshelf. "Make it easy on yourself, kid. Come out with your hands up," he hollered.

A low, buzzing sound filled the room, and a bluish light flashed across the ceiling tile.

Jasper jumped into the aisle "Gotcha!"

No one was there!

*What the h—! Where did they go?* The bookshelves rose to meet the ceiling. There was no way out. *I could have sworn I saw the kid.*

# CHAPTER 10

# ELSA WORTHINGTON

Bus #3 from Kingston pulled up to the main entrance of Franklin Hall. Bill Crow exited the bright yellow motor coach a little embarrassed, as he was the only upper classman on the bus. His mother forbade him riding to school with any of the other boys, especially Chad.

As soon as he entered the school, Bill immediately ran into Rico Steel, who appeared to be waiting for him. He hurried past the troublemaker.

"Hey, Crow, wait up!"

Bill kept walking.

Rico hollered again, "Bill, wait up."

Against his better judgment, Bill stopped.

Rico grabbed Bill's shoulder, but Bill hit his hand away. "What do you want?" he asked with contempt in his voice.

Rico backed off. "I know we're not tight, but I think it's wrong the way your friends treat you."

"Since when do you care about me?" Bill walked away.

Rico called after him. "How's it feel to be left out?"

Bill turned back with a scowl on his face. "What are you talking about?"

"You were the only one missing from your little clique."

Bill's patience was wearing thin. "Okay, I'll bite. Missing from what?"

Rico laughed. "The big adventure, what else?"

Bill waved him off and quickened his pace down the hall toward his locker. *What a jerk!*

Rico raced to catch up. "Geez, even I was invited."

By this time, Bill was rather annoyed. "Just spit it out...whatever it is you have to say."

"Your friends went on an amazing trip, and you weren't included. Can I make it any more plain to you?"

Bill stood with a suspicious look on his face. "What're you scheming now, Steel?"

Rico ignored Bill's remark. "It was some trip. I was surprised you weren't there until I overheard Chad say you'd be a drag."

As if on cue, Chad walked out into the hall. "Bus finally got here, huh," Chad called to Bill.

"There's your so-called friend. If you don't believe me, ask him." Rico scurried up the hall and watched from a distance.

Chad marched toward Bill. "Hey, are you coming to the Brotherhood meeting tonight?"

Bill stood at his locker. "Probably," he said as he tinkered with the combination lock.

Chad pointed up the hall. "What'd that loser want?"

"Nothing." Bill opened his locker and picked up his civics book.

"It looked intense. Was he bugging you?"

Bill leaned against his locker. "It's not worth mentioning."

"Try me."

"It's stupid. He said you guys went on an adventure without me. He'd say anything to cause trouble."

Bill turned around and detected a guilty expression on Chad's face. "Tell me he's lying," he said, with a sick feeling in the pit of his stomach.

Chad said nothing. A look of upset swept over his face.

"I don't believe it!" Bill slammed his locker door. "We're supposed to be best friends...and I had to hear it from Rico Steel of all people."

"It wasn't my idea. Josh swore me to secrecy."

"Yeah, blame Josh. It's never your fault."

"It wasn't even up to me to invite you." Just then, Josh appeared in the hall. Chad waved to him and said, "Ask him. He'll tell you."

"I don't care that I was excluded. I know most of the guys in the Brotherhood think I'm a jerk. I'm mad because you didn't trust me enough to tell me about it."

Tongue-tied, Chad finally said meekly, "I'm sorry."

"Some friend you are." Bill rushed to his homeroom without looking back.

Chad gritted his teeth and walked toward Rico. In a split second, Rico took off down the hall.

Josh grabbed Chad's shoulder in the nick of time.

"Let go of me."

"No way. I saw that look in your eyes," Josh said. "You'll get expelled if you fight Rico here. We can always get even off school property."

"That rotten son of a b—"

"Cool down, he's not worth the aggravation."

*Why didn't I tell Bill? I know he would have kept his mouth shut.* Chad felt as if someone had punched him in the gut. "When I get my hands on Rico, I'm going to pound the crap out of him."

"Don't worry; we'll get even with him. Brian won't be—"

Chad groaned and punched the wall. "This has nothing to do with Brian." He turned around and looked Josh in the eyes. "Rico told Bill about Paragon."

Josh swallowed hard. "Oh shoot, we forgot about Rico."

"You and your effin' secrecy. I should have told Bill myself as soon as we got home. But no, I listened to you…and now I may have lost my best friend."

Josh said, "Let me talk to him. I'll try to get him to understand."

"You've done enough damage. It's my problem. I'll solve it. I should've never listened to you guys in the first place." Chad abruptly left Josh standing alone in the hallway.

Bill ignored Chad all day. At lunch, he actually got up and left their table when Chad sat down to join the group. Passive aggression was Bill's forte. So after school, determined to make things right with his best friend, Chad stopped by the Crow residence. He stood at the mailbox in front of Bill's house to gather his thoughts, and then slowly made the trek up the driveway to the front porch.

Bill was the first kid Chad had met when the McGuires moved to Kingston four years earlier. From the start, Chad could see they were total opposites. But for some strange reason they clicked. Maybe it was because each admired the other's qualities. No one could figure it out, least of all Chad. One thing he knew—he had to settle this rift with Bill.

Chad knocked on the sturdy wooden door.

Someone pulled back the curtain in the living room bay window and peered out. Seconds later, the doorknob turned.

Needless to say, Chad groaned when Bill's mother, Elvira Crow, stood inside the opened door. He plastered a fake grin on his face. "Is Bill home?" he asked, knowing full well his friend probably stood within earshot.

"William is doing his homework and cannot be disturbed."

"Please tell him I stopped by," he said politely, almost choking on the words. Before Mrs. Crow could close the door, he added, "It's important that you tell him I was here. We have to settle something."

She sneered at Chad. "Of course, I'll tell him."

He detected the glint in her eyes and suspected she relished the fact he and Bill were feuding.

Mrs. Crow slammed the door.

Chad looked down, disappointed. He had wanted to get this misunderstanding settled today. An unexpected loud noise got his attention. A beat-up RV climbed the steep Kingston Club Road with difficulty. The vehicle looked like it had been through a war. The engine made a sharp, grinding noise. To Chad's amazement, the RV pulled into the Crow driveway. It stopped suddenly, producing a large backfire and a plume of smoke from under the hood.

A plump old woman dressed in a flowered muumuu got out of the driver's side and kicked the RV's front tire. "You piece of crap. I just put a fortune into you, and now you're going to act up?"

Chad chuckled at the woman's behavior, but he felt she couldn't have picked a worse place to break down. Sure that Mrs. Crow was on the phone calling the police at that precise moment, he thought, *I better warn her to move her camper.*

The old woman peered toward the house and then yelled out, "Is that you, Billy Boy?" She dashed up the walk, moving pretty well for someone her age and size. With an odd look on her face, she mumbled, "You're not Billy."

"No, ma'am. My name's Chad." He spied something around her neck—a peculiar necklace. A closer inspection revealed the necklace to be a bottle opener, hanging from a thick stainless steel chain. *Cool. I like this lady.*

The old lady gave Chad a spontaneous hug. "It's nice to meet you, Chad. My name is Elsa Worthington. My eyes aren't as good as they used to be. I thought you were my—"

"What are *you* doing here?" a voice squawked. Mrs. Crow stood on the small porch. Her eyes actually bulged, and the color had faded from her face, while her lips trembled. She pointed at the old woman. "What are you doing here?" she asked again.

Chad felt sorry for Elsa. Mrs. Crow would certainly make the old woman pay for having the nerve to park her broken-down RV in their driveway. Tempted to interfere, he wisely stood silent.

Elsa peered around Chad and waggled one forefinger at Mrs. Crow. "Now, is that any way to greet your mother?"

Chad laughed heartily.

Elvira Crow frowned at him. "Don't you have something to do, young man? I'll tell William you stopped by."

Oh, how Chad wanted to stay to get the full story on Elsa Worthington, but he had to meet Josh and the others at the tree house. He scooted down the sidewalk and headed toward the Monroe farm. He looked back and saw Mrs. Crow and her mother in the middle of an animated discussion.

Quite distraught, Elvira said, "I told you to call first before you paid a visit. And why, for gosh sake, did you have to drive that run-down RV?"

"Ol' Bessie? You complain I invade your space when I visit. I figured I'd stay in my RV while I was here. That way, I wouldn't clutter your precious house."

Elvira scanned the neighborhood. "Hurry up, get inside. I can't imagine what the neighbors must be thinking."

"It's good to see you too," Elsa said with a slight grunt, as she stepped into the foyer. "Well, your home is as neat as ever… I'll give you that." She walked down the short hall and peeked into the living room. "Yep, everything in its place."

Elvira moaned audibly.

"Is my grandson home?"

"He's studying and cannot be disturbed."

"We'll see about that." Elsa walked to the stairwell. "Hey, Billy Boy, it's Grandma," she hollered.

"So how long do you plan to stay?" Elvira asked sharply.

Elsa sighed. "That's what I love about you, darling. Your hospitality is legendary."

"It came out the wrong way. I just need to know so I can plan meals."

"You know me. I'll probably hang around till the wind changes." Elsa stared angrily at her daughter. "Besides, I want to get reacquainted with my grandson. It's been almost a year since I last laid eyes on him."

Elvira poked her finger at her mother. "Don't give me that look. I'd bring him around more, but it's tough to get away. I can't just take off from work anytime I please."

Elsa shook her head. "Yeah right, like Morgantown's on the other side of the world."

Within seconds, Bill bounded downstairs. His fun and free-spirited grandma was here! His feet pounded the hardwood steps as he rushed toward her.

"Grandma! Grandma!" He lunged into the old woman, practically knocking her over.

"Slow down, cowboy." She laughed. "You're the bright light of my day. Let me look at you… My, you've grown at least a foot since I've seen you last."

"I never get to see you anymore," he said.

Elsa frowned at her daughter.

"Well, at least your timing is good. Dinner will be ready within the hour," Elvira said, before disappearing into the kitchen.

Bill spotted the twinkle in his grandma's blue eyes. "So what brings you all the way from Morgantown?"

She gave Bill a kiss on his forehead. "Do I need a reason to visit my favorite grandson?"

Bill grinned. "I'm your only grandson."

"Well, you'd still be my favorite, even if I had twenty."

She didn't fool Bill. "Grandma, what really brought you here?"

"I just decided to take a little trip. I was getting bored at home."

"What's up?" he asked with a smirk.

She pulled her grandson close and whispered, "I could never fool you. Are you using your gift?"

"It's tough with Mom hovering over me."

"That's what I figured." She lowered her voice even further. "I did a reading yesterday and was shocked by what I saw. Are you still friends with the Monroe brothers?"

Bill rolled his eyes. "I guess... Why?"

"They're in terrible danger!"

# CHAPTER 11

# SKELETON KEYS

Mitzi Martel stood in front of the large mirror in the girls' lavatory. She applied a new coat of lip gloss with precision while Brittany Benton stood near the sink, fluffing her hair. Mitzi squinted. *Is that a zit!* Her heart fluttered as she moved closer to the mirror. Turning to her right to make sure Brittany wasn't watching, she quickly applied a dab of foundation to cover up the imperfection.

"Have you talked to Josh about the dance?" Brittany asked.

"No," Mitzi said harshly, surprised by the question.

"I thought you guys were going to be exclusive?"

Mitzi didn't like Brittany's grilling, not one bit. "Well, if you must know, we're not an item...yet," she said, staring into the mirror. "But we will be. We'll be going steady by the time the Halloween dance rolls around. You can bet on it."

She stealthily placed the small vial of foundation in her makeup bag and snapped it shut. The loud pop bounced off the ceramic tiles. "I've been busy, and so has he. Besides, I'm playing hard to get."

"Don't play too hard to get," Brittany said. "I heard from Emma Whitson, who heard it from Jess Parsetti, that he has a thing for Katie O'Hara... And he didn't exactly fall all over you the other day."

"Really! What's wrong with you? She's just a freshman." Mitzi cocked her head to the side. "Josh has his standards, or have you forgotten?"

"Well, I'm just telling you what I heard."

Mitzi smacked her lips together, pleased with her handiwork. "Josh always was a sucker for losers, and Katie O'Hara's a loser with a capital L. He's just being nice. I'm sure she's his new project. He'll get bored, trust me."

Just then, Dani Halverson strolled into the bathroom.

Mitzi spun around to face both girls. "I've been after Josh for three years. There's no way I'll let *anyone* steal him away...especially a dorky freshman." She turned back toward the mirror and smiled with satisfaction at her reflection. "So, are you girls ready to rock this place?"

Mitzi strutted out of the bathroom with Brittany and Dani in tow. No one, except for Josh Monroe, even came close to their coolness, according to her way of thinking.

Unfortunately, walking straight toward them were Katie and Sydney.

Mitzi whispered, "Oh, this will be fun." As the three cheerleaders passed by the two freshman girls, Mitzi stuck her foot out and tripped Katie.

Katie hit her knees hard. Her books scattered the full width of the hall. Katie seethed, sprawled out on the terrazzo floor. "What's your problem?"

Mitzi sneered at her. "Let's go, ladies. We don't want to catch anything from her."

Katie blurted out, "You're so pathetic! You're not worth the energy to—"

Brittany grabbed Katie by the hair and yanked her head back. "Do you know who you're talking to?"

Katie cowered. She looked down without saying another word.

"Good! Just make sure you remember where you stand in this school," Brittany said with a smirk.

As the three divas walked away, Dani turned around and glanced at Katie. Was that a look of compassion in her eyes?

Sydney bent down and helped Katie gather her books. "Those girls are evil."

Katie stood up, embarrassed but not broken. "I just hope Josh doesn't fall for their garbage."

The new librarian, Miss Beatrix "Bea" Butterfield, raced across the commons toward Pear Memorial Library. Her favorite pale-blue dress rustled as Bea sped across the sidewalk, while her shoulder-length blond hair blew in the wind. Though she usually sported a calm demeanor, today she was quite upset—late coming back from lunch—thanks to Mr. Werner! *That man's stories are so interesting.* A vision of students standing three deep outside the entrance of the library bounced around in her head, but there was no line. When Bea tried the door, she found it unlocked.

Flustered, Bea rushed inside and shouted sharply at the first person she saw. "How did you get in here?"

The startled girl stiffened. "Through the door," she said quickly.

"Don't get smart with me, young lady! Who let you inside?"

"I'm sorry, Miss Butterfield. The door was open and the lights were on. I just assumed you were in your office."

Bea took a deep breath. *Who unlocked the door?* "Carry on," she said, waving the girl away. She continued on to her desk. As she was about to check her e-mails, Bea noticed a small package sitting near her computer. *That's odd—UPS and FedEx usually deliver in the morning.*

Bea picked up the package and read the label. "What!" she mumbled. "Why in the world was this delivered here?" Bea looked up and saw Katie O'Hara and Sydney Mason enter the library.

"Miss O'Hara, may I have a word?"

Katie sauntered toward the counter. Her body language screamed loudly that she was no fan of the new librarian, which did not escape Bea. "Yes, Miss Butterfield?"

Bea held the small package. "I don't know who you think you are, young lady." She could see genuine confusion on the girl's face. "This is for you. It was on *my* desk." Bea handed the package over the counter. More precisely, she tossed the item at Katie.

"Who's it from?" Katie asked.

"I'm sure I don't know. But this had better not happen again. This is a library, not a post office!"

Both girls snickered as they walked toward their favorite reading desk. Katie took her seat at the broad wooden table and looked at the small package.

"What's her problem?" Sydney whispered, looking back at the librarian.

Katie shrugged. "She just doesn't like me. Believe me, the feeling's mutual," she said, quite emphatic with the last part.

This elicited a loud *Shh* from Miss Butterfield.

Katie pulled the brown wrapper off as quietly as she could, but the sound of tearing paper carried throughout the library. She looked toward the checkout desk. Miss Butterfield showed her disapproval by clenching her jaw. "Sorry," Katie whispered.

Amid the torn wrapping paper lay a plain cardboard carton; inside sat a tiny metal box, the type that typically held a small piece of jewelry.

Katie gulped. *Oh God! What if it's another enchanted ring?*

Sydney poked her. "Open it. I want to see what's inside."

Although Katie was not sure whether to open it or toss the small container into the nearest trash, curiosity finally got the best of her. The lid snapped open with a loud pop. She looked up, expecting to see a scowl on Miss Butterfield's face, but the librarian was not at the counter.

"What's in it?" Sydney asked impatiently.

Katie squinted. "Three keys. One's so old…it's rusty."

Sydney gave her a strange look. "I thought it'd be a ring."

"Wait, there's a note." Katie opened the folded piece of paper. It read: *These will come in handy when you least expect it.* She quickly grabbed the wrapping paper. Yep, it was addressed to her. But there was no return address. "Weird. Who would send me these?"

Sydney shrugged. "It's probably one of the boys trying to punk you. I wouldn't put it past Zach."

Katie nodded. "You're right. He thinks he's so cool" She shoved the box of keys into her backpack and opened her algebra book.

Katie lived across the road from Matt, so that night when she saw him tinkering near the barn, she decided to see if he knew anything about the keys.

"Are you sure you should be working?" Katie asked, as she joined him at the corncrib.

"I'm just goofing off a little," Matt said, shoveling feed into a bucket. "What's up?"

Katie showed him the small jewelry box. "Do you know anything about this?"

"What's inside?"

"Don't act so innocent." Katie handed him the box. "You put this on Miss Butterfield's desk, didn't you?"

Matt shook his head.

"You swear you had nothing to do with this?"

"It wasn't me." Matt popped the lid open and spied the three keys. "Skeleton keys? What are they for?"

"I have no clue."

Matt leaned on the shovel. "Strange things have been happening, and now you get an anonymous package containing three old skeleton keys."

Katie's stomach fluttered. "Creepy, huh?"

"It's just like when I found the ring. Only this time you're the lucky winner."

"Gee, thanks. You always know how to cheer me up."

Matt looked at his phone. "Oh crap, I have to run," he said, handing the keys back to Katie. "We're going out to dinner tonight with the Roundtrees."

As Matt ran toward the house, Katie called out to him. "You tell Zach, if he sent me the keys, I'll pay him back…with interest."

Matt looked back. "Zach's not that stupid. He knows not to get on your bad side."

Katie had to agree. But if Matt or Zach hadn't sent her the keys, who had?

CHAPTER 12

# NEW NEIGHBORS

Matt enjoyed Saturday mornings because of the scrumptious breakfasts his mother always prepared, and today was no exception. The smell of fresh waffles and bacon filled the house.

In the middle of breakfast, there was a knock on the kitchen door. Chad and Brian McGuire stood in the breezeway.

"Come on in, boys. Did you eat?" Kay Monroe asked.

Matt marveled at her transformation. Only a short month ago, his mother had disliked the two brothers intensely...and didn't hide the fact. But since their experience in Paragon, she had totally changed her attitude toward them.

"We had a little cereal," Chad said.

She pointed to two open chairs at the table. "Sit. That's no breakfast for two growing boys."

Without a word from either brother, plates of bacon and waffles were set in front of them, along with two glasses of orange juice.

Chad picked up a piece of bacon. "Is Josh ready?" he asked between chews.

"He'll be down," Frank Monroe said. He lowered the morning paper from his eyes. "So where are you guys going, anyway?"

"Ohiopyle," Brian said. "We're kayaking with a group of Eagle Scouts from Connellsville."

Matt thought about how much fun it would be to join them. But Josh, with help from Brian, had been delivering his papers since the panic attack. Now that he was deemed healthy, duty called—no kayaking for him. "Bring back some fudge," Matt said. "I don't know what they put in it, but it's the best I've ever tasted." He looked over at his mom. "Except for yours," he quickly added.

Chad grinned at Matt. He mouthed, "Suck-up."

Matt's face reddened. He shrugged and then whispered, "What can I say? I'm no dummy."

Josh bounded down the back stairs like a stampeding herd of buffalo. Floorboards popped with each step. He dashed into the kitchen, quickly kissed his mom on the cheek, sat at the table, and sucked up his breakfast like a human vacuum cleaner. After a loud belch, he jumped up and slung his duffle bag over his shoulder.

Matt snickered, while his mother groaned.

Frank looked up from his paper. "Do you need any money?"

"Thanks, Dad, I'm good," Josh said as he grabbed the small cooler near the door. Kay had packed it with snacks. Chad opened the screen door, and Josh stepped into the breezeway. "Sport, do you want anything from the trading post?"

Matt smiled. "Just a box of—"

"Fudge, right? What kind?"

"Peanut butter...but any flavor will do. Just so it's not sugar-free."

Josh nodded. "Got it."

"Fudge?" His father shook his head. "Of all the souvenirs in Ohiopyle, you pick fudge? I can't believe you're a dentist's son."

His mom patted Matt on the back. "Well, he gets it from me. Neither of us can get enough sugar."

Now that they were alone, Matt figured this was a good time to tell his parents about the skeleton keys. "You know when I found the ring and tablets I didn't tell you, and I promised to keep you in the loop if anything weird happened in the future, so—"

"Why don't I like the sound of where this is going?" his mother said. She plopped into the chair beside Matt.

"Something weird happened at school yesterday," Matt said. "Someone dropped off a strange package for Katie in the library."

"Who left it?" his father asked.

There was a knock at the screen door. It was Katie. Her timing couldn't have been any better. She stepped into the kitchen. Kay jumped up and asked, "Did you eat breakfast?"

"Oh yes, Mrs. Monroe. I'm full."

Matt pulled out a chair for his friend. "I was just telling Mom and Dad about the package you got yesterday."

Katie scowled. Obviously, she wasn't ready to share the news.

Matt couldn't believe her reaction. "Look, keeping everything a secret last time nearly got us killed. I wanted to see if they knew anything about the keys."

"What keys?" his mother asked, sitting down beside Matt.

Matt nudged Katie.

"Someone left a package for me in the library." Katie appeared frazzled; her voice cracked. "At first, I thought I opened it by mistake, but my name was on the—"

Matt grew impatient. "The box contained three old skeleton keys."

"Dr. Monroe, do you know what they could be for?" Katie asked nervously.

Frank scratched his head. "I have no idea."

"Are you sure, Dad?" Matt asked. "If there's something you know, you have to tell us."

His father tapped Matt lightly on the head with the newspaper. "What? Do you think every package or strange object has a secret behind it?"

"Well...well, hasn't that been the case lately?"

"I'm serious, Son. I have no idea what the keys are for," his dad said, with a slight chuckle.

Katie sighed. It was a deep sigh of frustration. "I was hoping you knew something. I guess Sydney was right. I've been punked."

Matt laughed. "Anyone who knows you wouldn't have the guts to do that."

Katie sat up straight and gasped. "I think I know who it was! Thanks, Matt." She jumped up, and in a split second she was out the door.

"Who?" Matt yelled. Too late—Katie was gone.

It had been almost two weeks since Matt had last delivered papers, and he was ready to get back into the swing of things. He looked forward to hearing the latest gossip from his neighbors. It wasn't long before Matt stopped in front of the Crow residence.

He rode his bike up the concrete driveway and noticed the dilapidated RV. Matt beamed when he saw the West Virginia license plate. *Grandma Elsa must be visiting*, he thought happily. When Elsa Worthington had lived in Kingston, all the kids called her Grandma Elsa, and Matt still thought of her that way. With renewed energy, he bounded up the front steps and rang the doorbell.

Mrs. Crow opened the door. "You Monroe boys are quite punctual. I could set my clock by your delivery. You are to be commended, Matthew."

To Matt, Elvira Crow was the only woman in Kingston who was more peculiar than his mom. She wasn't one of his favorite people, but she'd actually been decent to him since he started the paper route.

"Thank you, Mrs. Crow. I'm collecting today, and your bill is—"

"Six dollars, right?"

She may have been excessively stuffy, but Matt had to hand her one thing—the lady was efficient.

He gave her the newspaper and punched the payment card. "See you later," Matt said, as he hurried down the steps. He looked back at the front picture window and wondered if Bill was still mad at him for excluding him from the Brotherhood's journey to Paragon. Actually, he couldn't blame the kid.

"Paperboy."

Matt looked up and saw a chubby old woman walking toward him. It *was* Grandma! He practically flew over to her. "Grandma, how are you?" he asked, giving her a big hug.

Elsa Worthington squinted quizzically. "Matty, is that you?"

"Yep."

She threw her hands in the air. "My, have you grown."

Matt couldn't hide his excitement. "It's so good to see you." He gave her another big hug and grabbed her right hand. "I've missed you."

The old woman jumped back and gasped. Matt saw fear and confusion in her eyes.

Grandma Elsa shook her head as if coming out of a daydream. "Forgive me. Just a senior moment." She hesitated, and then said, "The reason I called out to you is I'd like to get a paper."

"I never turn down a new customer," he said with a wink. Matt handed her a *Latrobe Bulletin*. "I always carry an extra paper just in case. I'll start you off on Monday. You can cancel anytime."

Grandma Elsa appeared dazed. Matt jumped on his bike and waved as if everything was okay, but he was concerned. She waved back halfheartedly.

As Matt continued his ride up Kingston Club Road, his mind traveled from one subject to another, but it kept coming back to Grandma Elsa. *Why's she in Kingston? Is she sick? Maybe that's the reason she acted so out of it.*

Matt loved Bill's grandmother because she was unconventional. Grandma called herself a spiritualist—but certainly not the kind he had heard about in church. She seemed to have more faith in tarot cards than the Bible.

Deep in his daydreaming, he almost missed the turn into Dr. Payne's estate and had to slam down on his handbrakes. He lost control for a split second. The tires slid sideways on the fine gravel that covered the old macadam road, but he was able to recover his balance and made the turn into the driveway.

He pedaled up the lane. Soon the mansion came into view. The lawn had been mowed! The windows were clean, and the house had a fresh coat of paint. *Holy crap*, he thought. *What's going on?*

Matt noticed a young boy and girl playing on the porch. They waved at him.

He got off his bike and walked toward the porch. "Hi, I'm Matt," he said as he studied the two children. "I'm the paperboy."

The little girl giggled and ran behind her brother.

"Nathaniel…Nathaniel Parker," the boy said clearly as he extended his hand in friendship. "This is my sister, Annabelle."

"Nice to meet you," Matt said. "You're new to the neighborhood, aren't you? Where do you live?"

The boy crooked his neck, and his sister giggled again.

"We live here," Nathaniel said forcefully.

"This mansion? Really? I didn't realize it was sold."

"What do you mean?" Nathaniel's face wore a puzzled look. "We've lived here all our lives."

"That's impossible!" Matt blurted out. Impossible because Dr. Payne had lived in the mansion for as long as Matt could remember, and as far as he knew the old dentist didn't have any children or grandchildren.

Nathaniel gave Matt a stern look. "I ought to know where I live." The boy sounded sincere and a bit angry. "Would you like to come inside? I'll show you my room."

Matt agreed to go with him. *The game is on!*

Nathaniel opened the front door, and Matt followed him inside. The parlor was immaculate, not one spot of dust. The furniture looked brand-new; gone were the old horsehide sofa and the high-back chairs. They had been replaced by a Victorian-style matching living-room suite. The long velvet curtains opened wide, allowing sunlight to stream into the room. The wallpaper looked bright and clean. Matt could smell fresh paint.

"Wow, you really fixed this place up! I can't believe your family got this done so fast."

Annabelle finally spoke. "You're a silly boy."

Before Matt could answer, Nathaniel poked him and said, "Come on. Let me show you my room."

The boys rushed up the stairs, with Nathaniel leading the way. He pointed to the second door on the left. "That's my bedroom."

Like the parlor below, it was impeccably neat. Matt grinned; his room was a disaster zone compared to this bedroom. He and Josh were slobs.

Nathaniel walked to the window. "Look, I have a great view of the mountains."

This was the first time Matt had been upstairs in the old house. He peered out the bedroom window. The leaves on the large poplar and maple trees showed tinges of red and yellow mixed in with their familiar green. Matt could plainly see the ridges in the distance, glistening in bright sunlight. He envied Nathaniel the awesome view.

Every bit of space in the small room was used in such a way that the furniture did not clutter the area. A double bed with a brass frame, covered by a large quilt, dominated the bedroom. Matt recognized the quilt pattern—Pennsylvania Dutch. He had seen the design in an Amish shop when their family traveled to Smicksburg to buy furniture.

One thing Matt did find odd though—no computer on the desk, and no electronics in the room. The only thing Matt saw that proved it was a boy's room was a collection of toy soldiers on a bookshelf—Civil War era, Yankee and Rebel infantry.

"Your parents must be really strict," Matt said. He couldn't get over the lack of any technology.

Annabelle walked into the room and interrupted. "There's gingerbread cookies and cold cider in the kitchen."

The three bounded down the stairs. Matt bit into a cookie. "Wow, these are better than my mom's." He took a quick gulp of the apple cider. "Is this homemade?"

"You *are* a silly boy," Annabelle said once more.

Matt looked around the kitchen. "Neat. You have an old-fashioned icebox. That's so cool."

A door closed in another part of the house. Nathaniel jumped and listened intently. He lifted his eyes up toward the ceiling.

Matt peered at Nathaniel. The boy had to be only a few years younger than him, probably around twelve. He had never seen either of them at the academy, so he assumed they attended Derry Township public schools.

"Do you go to Kingston School?"

Again the boy gave him an odd look. "No. Our nanny teaches us."

"Well, excuse me, I never met anyone with a nanny before," Matt said sarcastically.

Annabelle gasped. "You don't have a nanny?"

Matt found her question peculiar. "No. But I'm too old for one anyway."

Nathaniel snorted. "I've been telling Mama I'm too old for a nanny, but she shrugs me off."

Suddenly a door slammed in another part of the house.

Annabelle dropped her cookie. She looked nervously at Nathaniel. "It's him. He's home!"

Matt noticed the tone of dread in her voice and the look of panic on her face.

Nathaniel jumped up from the table. "You have to go. We're not allowed to have visitors when our parents are out."

They quickly walked Matt to the front door.

"If you want me to introduce you to the other kids in the neighborhood, I'll be glad to," Matt said sincerely as he stepped onto the front porch.

"That won't be necessary," Nathaniel answered.

Annabelle begged her brother. "But Nathaniel, it would be so nice to make new friends."

He turned to his sister. "That's impossible." Nathaniel lowered his voice, but Matt heard him say, "Papa would never allow it."

"Well, if you change your mind, let me know," Matt said. "Tell your parents I'll bring you a complimentary *Latrobe Bulletin* on Monday."

Annabelle waved. "Goody, see you Monday."

Matt pedaled down the lane. As he neared the end of the driveway, he hit his brakes hard. *Surely they removed the portal before selling the house!*

CHAPTER 13

# REVELATION

Bill strolled across the driveway to his g
tapped on the door and entered.

The old woman sat at the kitchen
small side window. Her white hair shimmered i
which filtered through the tiny pane of glass. Sl
and smiled, although it was a weak smile. Her

Bill knew the look; something had her spo

"Sit down, Billy," Grandma said nervously, pa
her. "I have some news to share with you."

"What's wrong?" he asked, rushing to her si

"I talked with Matt Monroe earlier today."

"I don't want to hear anything he had to say

"Sit down and listen!"

Bill hadn't heard that tone from her in
quickly obeyed.

Grandma gave him a cross look. "If you had
you would know the boys had no option to tak
journey."

Bill shifted in the chair. "How did you know

"That's not important. What *is* important is w
to join them."

"I really don't care," Bill said, looking down.

'ho do you think you're talking to, young man?" She pursed her sn't that exactly what's bothering you?"

›ose bumps popped out over his entire body. *How does she do that?*

e've been blessed with a special gift, you and I," Grandma said. fference is I use my gift, while you squander yours." A look of ssion filled her face. "Look, I know your mother has made life lt for you."

l's eyes glistened with tears. "You don't understand how hard n. Mom goes ballistic every time I mention it," he said, quickly the tears from his eyes. "She says it's from the devil."

.bbish! That daughter of mine needs a good spanking," his nother said in a huff.

: thought of his mother bent over Grandma's knee, getting d, put a smile on Bill's face.

ing your gift will solve problems and bring contentment. And s the last thing the devil wants."

what did Matt say to you?" Bill asked, giving in to his grandmother.

thing."

t you said he—"

grabbed my hand and I saw his memories."

knew the meaning of her words, because he too could see memories; with a simple squeeze of their hands, their energy be imprinted on his soul. He never shook hands either in ulations or friendship, fearing the transfer of that person's ies; instead, he patted them on the shoulder.

grandmother reached out her hands. "Don't be afraid. Let ell you why you were excluded."

ing a deep breath, Bill grabbed his grandmother's withered nstantly, energy transferred to him. Memories flooded his Matt's memories.

saw Matt and Josh Monroe in their bedroom, lying on their ll heard Matt say, "I don't know why we can't tell our friends oing on."

Josh grunted. "I don't either. But Dad said it's a secret that can't be shared with anyone or there will be bad consequences."

"I know, but I feel terrible not telling the other guys."

The scene changed in Bill's mind. Now he saw the Monroe brothers, Katie O'Hara, and Zach Roundtree standing in a large basement filled with well-dressed adults. Matt held a strange set of wooden tablets and wore a glowing golden ring on his right hand.

Matt read from the tablets. "One day the ring shall be lost, the next day found. To the oath he is bound. The child it seeks shall be the finder."

Everyone in the room murmured. Then Bill saw Dr. Agregeous Payne motion for Matt to continue. Bill shuddered. *Why are they there with old Dr. Payne?*

"Welcome, Chosen One. You are the bearer of the promise," Matt read. A barrage of gasps, moans, and general bedlam followed his announcement.

"There's a final test," Dr. Payne yelled as he walked closer to Matt. "Matthew, remove the ring."

Matt tried to take the ring off his finger. It wouldn't budge.

Dr. Richard Steel sprang up out of nowhere. "To the oath he is bound," he said. "Ring to hand, hand to heart. Never are the two to part. Until the day evil falls, this child and sacred ring are one."

Dr. Payne walked toward Josh and the other teens. In a monotone, he said, "The other three are not free. To the oath they are bound. They must join the Chosen One in his quest as their forebears swore before them."

In the blink of an eye, Bill saw image after image flash in front of him, none more terrible than a huge fire-breathing dragon. That is, until a man dressed in black robes stood before him. The menacing red eyes of this terrible apparition burned into Bill's mind.

The last vision showed Matt and this man dressed in black, battling on top of a desolate mountain. Then all went dark.

Bill awoke on the small couch in the RV with a cold compress on his forehead. He sat up and looked around. His grandma, seated next to him, had a grave expression on her face.

"You gave me a fright!" she said in a shaky voice. After a deep sigh, she asked, "Now do you understand?"

Bill, damp with sweat, sighed. "Yeah, but what the heck happened to them?"

She answered in a scolding tone. "That's for you to find out."

Bill thought back to how mean he had been to the Monroe brothers and Chad. "Man, I owe them all an apology."

"You owe them nothing more than your friendship."

Bill stood up and walked to the door of the RV. "Thanks for setting me straight, Grandma. I can't wait to hear how they survived their ordeal."

"Stop… I have something else to tell you," she said firmly. "Their ordeal isn't over. When Matty grabbed my hand today, I sensed danger for him and all of Kingston."

Bill leaned against the door. "What?"

"Call the brothers and invite them here for dinner on Monday. I need to share something with them."

As Bill stepped out of the RV, his grandmother said, "I want you to join us. But don't let your mother know what's going on. She'll… she'll…oh, you know."

"You want *me* here?"

She propped the door open with her foot. "Yes. I'm not sure why, but I sense you'll play an important role in their next adventure."

Bill nodded. "That's good. At least I won't be left out this time."

*Oh, but you may wish you had been excluded, my dear.*

## CHAPTER 14

# CONFUSION

Matt parked his bike in the breezeway. His mother met him at the kitchen door. "Bill Crow's on the phone. He wants to speak with you."

Matt grabbed the phone from her. He took a deep breath and prepared himself for a verbal lashing. "Hey, Bill. What's up?"

However, Bill's voice was upbeat, almost friendly. "My grandma wants you and Josh to come to dinner on Monday night at six if that's okay. She said she'll order pizza."

"That's cool. We'll be there." *Should I bring up Paragon?* Matt bit his lip slightly. "Bill, I'd like to talk to you sometime about our trip and why you weren't included."

"You don't have to. I already know what happened," Bill answered abruptly.

Floored by this revelation, Matt asked, "Who told you?"

"You did."

"What?"

Bill hung up the phone without saying another word.

That night at dinner, Matt sat quietly, eating his ham and scalloped potatoes. It was a pleasant evening. "Mom, can you call the *Bulletin* office and tell them I'll need two extra papers on Monday?"

His mother looked up. "Did you get new customers?"

"Mrs. Worthington for sure, and—"

"I heard she was back in town. I should invite her to dinner before she goes back to West Virginia. She was always so kind to you boys."

"The other paper is for the people living in the Payne mansion," Matt said. He reached for the last piece of ham on the platter in the middle of the table.

His father raised his eyebrows. "Who?"

"The people living in the mansion. The old Payne estate must have been sold," Matt said. "Two kids were playing on the front porch. They said they live there."

Josh grunted. "I hope they didn't pay much for that old dump. They're going to have to spend a fortune fixing it up."

"Those kids were pulling your leg," his dad said. "Remember, Dr. Payne signed the estate over to me before he left town. I can tell you with certainty…the mansion hasn't been sold."

Matt swallowed a spoonful of potatoes. "Oh, they live there, Dad. At first, I thought the boy was kidding around too, but then he invited me inside the house. His parents really fixed the place up. You should see it. It's actually pretty nice." He reached for a piece of fresh-baked wheat bread.

Now it was his mother's turn to question him. "What are you talking about?"

"The place was immaculate. I went upstairs to the boy's bedroom. You'd love him, Mom. His room was spotless."

Matt could see the confusion on his parents' faces. "The boy said his name was Nathaniel."

Matt's father choked on a small piece of ham. "Who?"

Matt looked up. "Nathaniel…Nathaniel Parker."

"That's just not possible," his mom said, dropping her napkin.

Josh grumbled. "Who cares? So someone bought the old Payne estate or is renting it. What difference does it make?"

"It's not that simple." Frank's right hand shook as he wiped sweat from his forehead.

"Think about it, Frank," Kay said with a nervous tremor in her voice. "Matty has to be confused. It's just not possible. Maybe he didn't hear the boy correctly." Turning to Matt, she asked, almost pleading, "You must have misunderstood the boy. He didn't really say his name was Nathaniel Parker, did he?"

"What's the big deal?" Josh asked.

Matt looked at his mother quizzically. "I didn't misunderstand him. He said his name is Nathaniel Parker, and his little sister's name is Annabelle."

Kay slumped in the chair.

"Are you all right, Mom?" Josh jumped up to steady her.

"What's the big deal?" Matt asked.

His dad cleared his throat nervously. "Those kids were teasing you. They can't be the Parker children. As your mother said, it's just not possible...because Nathaniel and Annabelle Parker are dead."

CHAPTER 15

# The Parker Family

"Nathaniel and Annabelle Parker are dead," his father repeated.

"Oh, joy! I think I know where this is going," Josh said with a snicker.

Matt leaned back in his chair with flushed cheeks. "What? You're saying I talked with two dead kids today. They're ghosts?"

His parents gave Matt the most peculiar look.

"No way!" Matt exclaimed. "I touched them. They were flesh and blood. Dad, they were as real as you and me. Odd maybe, but real."

His father looked genuinely confused. "That's why they had to be teasing you."

Josh chuckled. "Sport, life is never dull with you around."

"I'm sure they were real," Frank said. "They just couldn't be Nathaniel and Annabelle Parker."

"I think those kids were cruel to you, pretending to be the dead Parker children," Kay said compassionately. She poked Frank. "Tell the boys the story about Nathaniel and Annabelle."

Frank leaned back in his chair. "The real Nathaniel and Annabelle Parker are definitely dead. They lived in the old mansion years ago. They were found beaten to death in the upper pasture of what is now the Sherman farm. Their stepfather, Colonel Parker, was suspected of the crime, but he was never brought to trial."

Josh jumped into the conversation. "I thought you said no one lived in the mansion except our relatives until it was sold to Dr. Payne."

Frank tapped his fingers nervously on the table. "It was rented out once…to Colonel Parker. We never mentioned it because of the gruesome murders."

Josh grunted.

"It was something we felt you didn't need to know," Kay said sharply.

Frank leaned forward and placed both elbows on the table. "That is, until now. At the time, everyone felt the stepfather killed the children. But he was never charged with the crime because there was no evidence to support the claim. The colonel committed suicide soon afterward—whether out of guilt or grief, no one knows for sure."

"Those kids are definitely scared of him," Matt said.

"Who is scared of who?" his father asked.

"Nathaniel and Annabelle. They're scared of their stepfather."

"I don't know who *those* kids are, but Nathaniel and Annabelle Parker lived over a hundred years ago," his mom said emphatically.

Matt paused to collect his thoughts. *Why won't they listen to me?* He pressed the point. "Whoever they are, they're definitely afraid of someone. Nathaniel made me leave when he thought his stepfather came home."

His mother sighed deeply. "That just doesn't make any sense. Those kids only pretended to be Nathanial and Annabelle."

"The place is all fixed up," Matt said. "The grass was mowed, and the outside of the house was painted."

In a raised voice, his mother said, "That can't be!"

Matt rolled his eyes. "Do you think I'm lying?"

Once again, his dad wiped sweat from his forehead. "All of Dr. Payne's furniture was removed, but the old house hasn't been cleaned yet. And the exterior certainly hasn't been painted."

"Well, somebody painted it. And obviously someone's moved in," Matt said in defiance.

"Who cares?" Josh burst out. "This is boring."

Kay looked pityingly at Matt. "Son, maybe you misunderstood what you saw."

"That property has *not* been sold," Frank said forcefully. "I know because—"

"So someone's renting," Josh said. "Big deal."

"No, Josh," Frank said. "No one's renting the house. The place is empty. It hasn't even been cleaned yet."

Matt crossed his arms and gritted his teeth. "I'm telling you, the house is clean, and it's full of new furniture."

His dad's face reddened. He threw his napkin onto the table. "I don't know what's going on. But we're going over there right now."

## CHAPTER 16

# ENIGMA

Frank Monroe and his sons stepped out of the car and walked toward the front of the mansion. The lawn had not been mowed; it stood over a foot high. Dried leaves blew across the wooden porch, while a rain gutter on the far left hung down, swinging in the wind. The faded cream-colored paint on the clapboard siding had bubbled and peeled, exposing bare wood. The bleak house looked as uninviting as ever.

"I thought you said this place was fixed up," Josh said crossly.

Matt stood rigid, with his mouth gaping. "I don't understand. This morning it looked great. The grass was cut, and the house was painted. Even the door was different. It had a large piece of glass on top, made out of different colors."

Frank took a large gulp of air. "Did it look something like a stained glass window in church?"

"Yeah, but where is it?" Matt's voice quavered.

"Dr. Payne had that door removed over thirty years ago," Frank said with raised eyebrows.

Josh slapped Matt on the back. "Are you sure you didn't overdose on your meds?" he asked, obviously still doubting him.

In no mood to be teased, Matt angrily pushed his brother away. "I'm not crazy. I know what I saw."

Their father pulled a large skeleton key out of his pocket. Matt saw it and shivered. It resembled a larger version of the skeleton keys

Katie had shown him. Frank placed the key in the keyhole on the left side of the door.

Matt observed the effort it took to turn the tumbler. The lock wouldn't turn, as though the door hadn't been opened for quite some time. But the door had opened easily for Nathaniel earlier that day. Matt's confusion ratcheted up another notch.

Frank struggled with the lock until the dead bolt finally turned with a loud click, and the door jumped open a little. He pulled on the doorknob. The loud screeching of the hinges could have awakened the dead. The light switch inside the door didn't work, so they left the door ajar to allow some light to filter into the house.

Frank stepped through the parlor over scattered papers and dust bunnies. His footsteps echoed across the hardwood floor. He opened the draperies, which allowed more light to enter the bleak, cold room.

Fear piled on top of Matt's confusion. *Am I getting sick again? Did I hallucinate the whole thing?* "I don't understand. It was clean this morning," Matt said anxiously.

Josh gave Matt a sour look. "You're full of—"

"Look!" their father shouted. He bent down and picked up a small baby doll dressed in vintage clothing. The doll appeared in mint condition, as though newly bought. "Where did this come from?"

Matt took a quick look. He breathed a sigh of relief. "Oh, that's the doll Annabelle carried around with her."

Kay gave her husband a quizzical look when he entered the kitchen. Frank walked over and gave her a little peck on the cheek.

"Well?" she asked.

Frank took a deep breath. "Oh, the house is empty, all right." He stalled for time by cleaning his eyeglasses. "But something strange is going on there."

"What do you mean?" Kay gnawed nervously on her lower lip.

"I could see Matty was really upset when we went inside."

"You don't suppose he's getting sick and just imagined all of it, do you?" Kay asked, anxiously.

"If he was hallucinating, can you explain this?" Frank showed her the doll.

"What's that?"

"We found it in the house."

Perplexed, Kay said, "But it looks brand-new."

"Yeah, that's the kicker. The house was a mess. But this little beauty was lying in the middle of the parlor floor."

Kay leaned back against the kitchen counter. "How is that even possible?"

Frank looked up to the ceiling and sighed. "Because I don't think Matty was hallucinating."

Kay's face lost its color. "What...what do we tell the boys?" she stammered.

Their sons entered the kitchen. "Tell us what?" Matt asked.

Kay flinched when she heard his voice.

"Everyone, let's sit and talk," Frank said, pulling back a wooden kitchen chair.

Kay set four pieces of German chocolate cake on the table. She winked at Matt as she placed an extra-large piece in front of him. "We didn't have time for dessert earlier."

"All right, Mom," Matt said with a huge smile.

"You and your sweets," Frank said, chuckling. After a quick sip of coffee, he looked directly at Matt. "I could see that you were upset when we stepped into the mansion."

Matt sat his fork down and leaned forward. "I'm telling you the house was clean this morning. I know what I saw."

"I want you to know, I don't think you were hallucinating." Frank placed a reassuring hand on Matt's arm.

"So you believe me?" he asked with the stirrings of hope in his voice.

"But the house was a mess," Josh said abruptly. "How could it be clean one minute and a mess the next?"

"This is going to sound strange," Frank said. "But I think Matty traveled into another time dimension."

Josh cringed. "Do you think the portal in the basement was opened somehow?"

"That wouldn't explain time travel. I think it's the ring that allowed your brother to travel back in time."

"Those kids were murdered," Kay said, looking caringly at Matt. "Maybe their souls are lingering in this plane, and somehow they were able to communicate with you."

"But where did the doll come from if they're ghosts?" Josh asked.

"That's a puzzler," Frank said as he wiped a smudge of icing from his upper lip.

Matt sat up straight. "Come to think of it, they were dressed in weird clothes."

Kay rubbed her chin. "That would make sense. If they are the real Nathaniel and Annabelle, they would be dressed like children from the early twentieth century."

"At least I'm not going crazy," Matt said with a big sigh. "Tonight, when I saw the house was a mess, I freaked… I thought I was getting sick again."

Out of habit, Kay jumped up and felt Matt's forehead. She smiled. "No fever."

"I'm going to see if I can reach King Darius. I want to know if he has any idea what could be going on," Frank said.

Josh pounded the table with a fist. Everyone jumped. "Sorry," he said, gritting his teeth. "But I remember… The king said Sport could attract all kinds of weird stuff for a while. Maybe this is what he was talking about."

Matt swallowed a large bite of cake. "It's been interesting, that's for sure."

Frank leaned back in his chair. "How am I going to get back to Paragon? If Leota were here, it would be a snap through the portal."

## CHAPTER 17

# Tarot Card Reading

Josh did not want to aggravate Mrs. Crow by parking in her driveway, so he pulled into the Kingston Sportsman Club parking lot to avoid a confrontation. Besides, it was a short walk from the hunting lodge to Bill's house. He put the car in park and turned off the engine. Releasing his seat belt, Josh said with a chuckle, "I can't believe Grandma Elsa is Elvira Crow's mother."

"Yeah, they're like night and day," Matt said.

"How can Grandma be so much fun, while her daughter is such an old prude?"

"It kind of makes you wonder," Matt said, looking over toward Josh.

"About what?"

"What Bill would be like if he had been raised by his grandmother."

"Good point," Josh said as he swung the car door open. "I'm sure he wouldn't be so uptight. But then again, she did raise Mrs. Crow."

The brothers stepped out of the Camaro and walked up the steep hill toward Bill's house. "I don't know what you said to Grandma, but thanks," Josh said.

"I didn't say anything to her," Matt said, kicking pieces of gravel as he walked.

"Bill's going to be there, isn't he?"

Matt shrugged. "I don't know. I didn't think to ask."

"At least he was a little friendlier at school today. But he still wasn't himself."

As they headed up the driveway, Bill popped out of the RV and waved them forward. "We're in here," he hollered.

The boys stepped inside the motor home. Grandma Elsa stood at the sink. She took a long look at Josh, and said cheerfully, "Oh my, you turned into such a handsome young man."

Matt groaned, while Bill rolled his eyes.

Josh hugged the old lady. "It's good to see you again, Grandma."

"Sit," she said. "What will you have to drink?"

Poker-faced, Josh said, "Beer will be fine with me."

Grandma chuckled. "Dream on, honey. Besides, I'd get shot by your mother." She rooted through the small refrigerator. "If memory serves me right, Matty likes Mountain Dew and you're a Coke fan." Grandma Elsa also took a cold bottle of beer from the fridge. "This is for me."

Matt grinned as the old woman popped the lids off the bottles with the opener that hung around her neck, even though they were twist-off caps. She was famous for that gizmo.

A light tapping on the door signaled the arrival of the pizza. "That was quick," Grandma said as she paid the driver.

She scattered napkins and paper plates around the piping hot pizza that now sat in the middle of the table. No one made a move to take the first piece.

Grandma sighed. "Dig in before it gets cold." She grabbed the first piece. "I remembered you boys like Jioio's pizza, so enjoy." She took a large gulp of Iron City beer.

Bill wiped his face with a napkin to remove a bit of sauce that had run down his chin. "Grandma, tell them what you know. I'm sure they're curious."

The old woman put her right hand in the air as she swallowed a bite of pizza. "I'm so happy to see you boys that I almost forgot why I asked you here."

Matt noticed a twinkle in her eyes.

Grandma said slowly and concisely, "I understand you went on an interesting trip recently."

The brothers sat up straight.

"Huh?" Josh asked.

"Don't worry, honey. Your secret is safe with me," she said with a wink.

A trickle of sweat ran down Matt's face, and Josh nervously took a large gulp of Coke.

"So how was Paragon?" Grandma asked coolly.

Josh choked. He tried to control his swallow, but he spit some of the Coke onto the paper plate in front of him.

Matt dropped his piece of pizza. "What? How do you know about Paragon?"

"Billy, tell them," Grandma Elsa commanded.

It was Bill's turn on the hot seat.

Grandma giggled like a little girl. "They aren't the only ones who keep secrets, are they?"

Bill's face turned pale.

"What's going on?" Matt asked.

"I have a special gift," Grandma Elsa said. "Billy inherited it from me. If he'd use it, he would have known about this much sooner."

Matt turned to Bill and scrunched his forehead. "What kind of gift?"

Bill struggled to speak. "It's a form of ESP… I can see people's memories." Immediately, he looked down at the table to avoid eye contact with the Monroe brothers.

"Then why didn't you know about our trip?" Josh asked, clearly irritated.

"I have to physically hold their hand, and then their memories flow to me," Bill said nervously, still looking down.

Matt snickered. "Man, that would be a great gift to have. If you want to know whether someone's lying, just grab them."

"It's not quite that easy." Bill looked Matt in the eyes. "It can drain your energy, and I have to be careful. It can wipe me out for days."

Bill's grandmother chimed in. "Billy's gift is rudimentary. He has to develop it. But my daughter's held him back."

"That's putting it mildly," Matt muttered, barely audible.

"What?" the old lady asked with a slight chuckle.

"The pizza's really good… I said the pizza's really good." Matt's cheeks flushed with embarrassment. Grandma shook a teasing finger at him.

"Matty, I understand you have a special gift too," Grandma said. "I know about the ring. May I see it?"

Totally surprised by the request, Matt held out his right hand.

Grandma moved closer to him and peered at the unique piece of jewelry. "It's beautiful," she said before taking another gulp of beer. Out of the blue, she asked, "You haven't been sleeping too well lately, have you?"

Matt stared at Grandma with wide eyes. She didn't give him time to answer. "Guess who my first crush was when I was a girl?" Grandma said excitedly, rubbing her hands together.

Matt didn't see the relevance of the question, but he thought he'd humor her. "Who?"

"Your great-grandfather!"

"Holy crap!" Josh shouted in amazement. "You've got to be kidding me. I didn't realize you even knew him."

"I was ten years old when I first met him at a 4-H cookout. He had just graduated from college. God…was he handsome. He looked a lot like you, Josh."

Matt tapped the table impatiently.

Grandma sat staring up at the ceiling, evidently lost in the past.

Bill patted her on the shoulder.

She jumped slightly, stirred from her fantasy. "He was my knight in shining armor."

Matt's patience had worn thin. "That's nice, Grandma. But what does—"

"I know he's alive," the old lady said with a sly grin.

Matt's jaw dropped.

"We communicate regularly. He's the one who told me about your recent escapades in Paragon."

Matt's mind went into overdrive. *If Dad can't contact Paragon, maybe Grandma Elsa can.* He blurted out, "You're here to help us, aren't you?"

Grandma leaned forward and squeezed Matt's cheek. "You always were the smart one. Let's do a reading to see how things will develop." She turned to Bill. "Honey, get the cards from the top of my bureau."

"Remember how we used the tarot cards when you were little kids?" she asked Matt. "Were they ever wrong?"

"No," Matt said vigorously.

"I thought I'd consult the tarot to see how you'll fare."

Bill returned with the cards. As soon as Matt saw the deck, memories of fun days gone by flooded his mind.

"Boys, since the events to come concern both of you, the reading will be inclusive. Both of you touch the cards." The brothers leaned forward and touched the top card.

"Good," Grandma Elsa said. She shuffled the deck. "Matty, you cut the cards," she commanded. Matt complied. Then she asked Josh to cut the deck. He followed her orders.

"We'll use the modified Celtic cross." Grandma laid the cards face down on the table. Matt instantly recognized the design. The first card she turned over was *death*. The brothers groaned in unison.

The old lady scowled. "Have you boys forgotten everything I taught you? The death card doesn't necessarily mean someone will die. It usually means great changes are ahead."

Matt nervously tapped the table. "I've had about as much change as I can handle for a while."

Grandma chided him. "Fate and karma are tied together in a neat little bow. We don't get to pick and choose."

The next card turned over was the *moon*. Grandma smacked her lips together. "This card means you'll have to go on without a clear picture of where you're going."

Josh grimaced. "That won't be hard, since we have no clue where all this is leading."

"That's just wonderful," Matt said in frustration.

"That's life, little one," Grandma said sympathetically. She then turned over the *devil* card. She looked directly at Josh and mirrored his grimace. "You and Matty must be very careful. Don't go against what you know to be right and true. You mustn't play a game with dangerous forces. Trickery will backfire."

The next card she turned over was *death*. Grandma jumped back as if she had been burned. "That's impossible. There's only one death card in the tarot." She stared angrily at Bill. "Did you mix two decks together?"

"No way," Bill said, defensively. "I didn't even know where you hid the cards until just now."

Rubbing the back of her neck, Grandma said, "This is odd. I knew you boys were in danger, but this reading is very strange. Let me remove this death card and start over."

Matt watched her count the cards.

Grandma sighed deeply and dabbed her forehead with a napkin. "Yes, there was an extra card in the deck. I don't know how that happened." She shifted in her seat. "Let me try a simpler reading."

She put the extra death card aside, reshuffled the cards, and had Matt and Josh cut the deck. The first card she turned over was *death*. Again the boys groaned in unison.

"Don't get excited," she said. "This only reaffirms that you are going to face great changes in your life." She turned over the second card. It was also *death*.

Matt was puzzled. "I thought there was only one death card."

Grandma leaned back in her chair. "This is not possible."

She slowly turned over the third card. It was *death* again! A look of terror filled her face. She stared directly at the brothers. "You must be extremely careful. You're facing very dark forces."

Josh laughed. It was a nervous laugh. "Come on, this is good fun, but I don't take it seriously. Do you, Grandma?"

"Absolutely! I believe in the tarot. There are many mysteries in life we don't understand, and the tarot is one vehicle used to decipher them."

Matt sat up in his chair. "Then this is not good."

Grandma Elsa placed her hands on the side of her face. "This is definitely not good...for you...or for anyone in Kingston."

"Gee, this has been fun," Matt said with a grunt. "We should do this more often."

Grandma snickered, and soon everyone laughed. "Don't lose that wonderful sense of humor," she said. She leaned forward and mussed up Matt's hair. "It will get you through the tough times."

Josh slapped his forehead. "I should have known something was up."

"Why do you say that, dear?" Grandma asked.

"King Darius told me to keep my eyes open. He sensed our troubles weren't over. He said opening the portal to Paragon could attract evil entities to Kingston."

Matt looked at Bill. "Are you sure you still want to join us?"

Bill smiled weakly. "You guys are in the Brotherhood. I have no choice."

## CHAPTER 18

# A TERRIFYING VISITOR

Matt flopped on his bed, totally exhausted. The evening with Bill's grandmother played back again and again in his mind. He didn't need Grandma to tell him something big was about to happen; he sensed it. He fell asleep for a few minutes, then awakened. This pattern continued all night long. At one point, Matt looked over to his brother's bed. It was empty. He assumed Josh was in the bathroom. His eyes grew heavy once more, and he slipped from consciousness.

In an instant, Matt opened his eyes and found himself sitting under a giant maple tree on the Payne estate; it was the one closest to the house in the column of trees lining the driveway. He heard light footsteps from behind, then a slight tap on his shoulder. Annabelle Parker stood there, giggling.

"What are you doing?" she asked with a lilt to her voice.

Matt appreciated the little girl's innocence. "Oh, just relaxing." He looked around. "Where's Nathaniel?"

"He's fishing at the pond."

"I wish he'd told me he was going. I would have joined him."

"Oh, he always fishes alone," Annabelle said quite seriously. "He says that's when he can think."

"I know what he means. Sometimes you need to veg out."

Annabelle scrunched her forehead. "What?"

Before he could answer, Matt heard a deep, harsh voice calling from the mansion. Immediately, Annabelle ran toward the porch, yelling, "I'm here, Papa, I'm here, Papa."

The man stood proud and straight on the top step that led to the large front porch. He looked out toward Matt, who still sat under the huge maple. "What are you doing here?" he yelled.

Matt got up and approached the mansion. "My name is—"

"Who said you could come here? You're trespassing. Get off my property."

"I just wanted to know if you wanted a newspaper. I'm the local paperboy." Matt continued his walk toward the porch.

"I said get off my property…now!"

Matt shivered—he recognized the man. He could not forget that menacing look—the look of a vicious dog. Colonel Parker was the man he had seen in the shed the other night!

The man grabbed little Annabelle by the arm and roughly lifted her onto the porch. "What did I tell you about talking with strangers? These village people are not to be trusted."

"Please don't hurt me."

Annabelle's words awoke something buried in Matt's subconscious. *It's her! Annabelle was the little girl in the shed that night.* Matt flinched when he heard a loud slap. Annabelle broke into piercing sobs. She darted inside the house.

A deep-red aura overtook Colonel Parker. Sensing evil, Matt knew it was time to leave. He'd tell his father about the episode.

Just then, Nathaniel appeared, strolling aimlessly up the driveway, fishing rod and bait can in hand. He seemed to be lost in thought until he spotted Matt. "Hi," he called innocently. He picked up his pace and rushed toward Matt.

A quick change in the boy's facial expression ensued when Nathaniel looked toward the front porch. The boy's eyes filled with terror.

Matt walked up to the frightened boy. "What's his problem, he's an—"

Nathaniel grabbed Matt. With his voice shaking, he said, "Quick, get out of here. Your brother's in great danger. Go to him."

"What do you mean he's in danger?"

Nathaniel ran to his stepfather. The man quickly grabbed the young boy, who dropped his rod and bait can. Colonel Parker pulled out a leather strap. Matt turned and looked away. He flinched at the horrendous whipping sounds.

Over the wails of his stepson, the man screamed, "What did I tell you? Never leave your sister alone!"

Matt sat up in bed. Sweat poured down his face. It was a nightmare. He looked over at Josh's bed. It was empty. Then he stared at his phone. It showed 2:40 a.m. Matt panicked. Was his brother sick again? He scurried to the hall bathroom. The door hung open, and the room was dark.

Matt threw on a pair of shorts and jumped into his sneakers. He tiptoed down the steps and looked around the first floor—no Josh. Matt grabbed a flashlight from under the kitchen sink. He ran to the tree house. "Josh, are you up there?" he called in a loud whisper. No answer.

By this time, Matt was imagining all sorts of bad scenarios. Maybe the infected wound had spread poison to Josh's brain, making him delirious. He regretted his decision to keep his brother's injury from their parents. In a panicked state, a sudden thought surfaced. *Maybe Josh walked to the ball field.*

Matt sped toward the creek. That's when he heard a loud screech. It echoed through the valley. The piercing sound caused goose bumps to pop out over his entire body. His adrenaline level spiked, and he practically jumped over the creek in one leap. His right foot hit the shallow part of the water, causing a loud splash.

Matt had taken this trail thousands of times before and sped through it, for he instinctively knew where to duck low branches and when to jump over exposed tree roots. He cleared the woods and stood on the edge of the baseball field.

"Josh," he yelled. "Where are you?" Matt walked toward the pavilion, and that's when he saw it—a large creature crouched down near one of the block pillars. It was too big to be a bear.

The creature sat up and stretched. Matt knew instantly what stood before him—a dragon! *How is this possible*, he thought. His heart pounded so strongly, he worried the menacing creature might hear the loud thumping.

The dragon was not as big as the one in Paragon, but nasty all the same. In a split second, it roared and took to the air. It flew directly at Matt, who dived to the ground. Unexpectedly, he heard gunshots. The dragon climbed the night sky and disappeared.

Matt looked over and saw Mr. Sherman. The old man held a shotgun. "It's me, Mr. Sherman. Matt Monroe," he hollered, waving his hands over his head.

The old farmer peered at Matt. "What the heck are you doing out this late? I could have shot you, boy."

"My brother is missing. Have you seen him?"

"No, I haven't, but did you see that thing? I've never seen anything like it."

How should he break the news to his neighbor? Matt decided to just blurt it out. "It was a dragon!"

"A what?"

Matt grabbed Mr. Sherman's arm. "I can't explain it now. But it was a dragon."

The old man stepped back. Even in the poor lighting, Matt saw the strange look on the farmer's face.

"Are you on drugs?"

Aggravated by the question, Matt snapped. "No…of course not."

The farmer placed the butt of the shotgun on the ground. "Well, whatever it was, my guess is it won't be back tonight. I got a good shot at it earlier. It was carrying a calf. I know I hit it, because it shrieked and dropped the calf. So I waited for it to cir—"

"Mr. Sherman, I've got to get home," Matt said urgently. He pinched himself to make sure he wasn't dreaming again; it hurt, confirming he was awake.

*How did a dragon get to Kingston? It had to come from Paragon.* Should he wake his parents? And where was Josh? All kinds of questions ran through his mind. He arrived at the creek. This time, he plowed through the water, soaking his shoes.

By the time he got to their backyard, Matt was panting for air. He bent over, trying to catch his breath. That's when he heard a moan, then a loud groan.

"Help," a voice called out.

It was Josh!

Matt whispered loudly, "Where are you?"

There was no answer.

Matt panicked. He yelled, "Where are you?" If he woke his parents, he'd face the consequences.

"Tree house," the voice said very weakly.

Matt quickly climbed the rope ladder. He looked into the small building and spotted a crouched form in the far corner. He shone his flashlight. It was Josh!

What little clothing Josh wore hung in shreds. His side bled excessively, and he shook uncontrollably. Josh looked up. *Dragon* was the only word he said.

"I'm getting Mom and Dad." Matt turned to go down the ladder.

Josh attempted to sit up. "Don't get them. Mom will freak," he whispered weakly.

What should he do? His brother obviously needed more help than he could offer.

Josh sat up. "Just help me into the house. I'm okay now."

"What happened? Was it the dragon?"

A bewildered look filled Josh's eyes. "Dragon? What dragon?"

"You said *dragon* when I climbed into the tree house. Don't you remember?"

"I don't know what you're talking about," Josh said with difficulty.

With Matt's help, Josh descended the rope ladder. They hobbled into the house and climbed the back stairs. Matt led Josh to the bathroom. No sooner had the door closed there was a rap on the bathroom door.

"Boys, what's going on?" their father asked.

Matt opened the door slightly. "Josh is sick. Must be the flu. He threw up, and I'm helping clean up." He quickly closed the door and locked it.

Frank pounded on the door.

"Dad, I can handle it," Matt said softly.

Josh fell to the floor with a thud.

"Open this door now!"

CHAPTER 19

# JOSH'S STORY

Frank heard the boys talking. "I said open this door...*now*!"

The door opened slowly. Matt peeked out with a frightened look on his face.

Frank pushed the door open and stepped into the bathroom. He pursed his lips. A mix of concern and anger spread across his face. "What are you guys up to?" he asked angrily. With one glance at Josh, his eyes widened. "My God! What happened to you?"

Not waiting for an answer, he lifted Josh and sat him down on the toilet.

Matt answered, "I'm not sure, Dad. I found Josh—"

"I wasn't talking to you," Frank said, crossly. He raised Josh's head and looked him in the eyes. "I asked you...what happened?"

Josh pushed his father's hand away and looked down at the floor. "I'm dizzy."

"Matty, get me a glass of water," Frank commanded.

Matt complied.

Frank handed the small paper cup to Josh. "Drink this," he said in a firm voice.

Josh looked dazed. Matt tried to speak up, but Frank motioned for him to be silent.

Josh said weakly, "I woke up, and it was really stuffy in our bedroom. I was having a rough time sleeping." He grabbed his side and moaned. "Matty looked like he was finally having a good night's sleep. I didn't want to wake him, so I decided to go outside and sit on the swing."

"What happened to your side?"

"It's the injury from Paragon. It hurts, but I'm okay."

Frank guided Josh to the sink. "I can't believe it's not healed yet." He grabbed the antibacterial ointment from Matt and then applied a bandage to Josh's open wound. After looking his son over, he said, "It looks like there's another cut on your left side."

As Frank applied the ointment, Josh moaned and sucked in his gut.

"Did that hurt?" Matt asked sympathetically.

Josh grinned a little, but quickly winced. "No. I just like to fake like I'm in pain." He turned toward the mirror, viewing his wounds. "Hmmm," he said. "How'd I get this one?"

Matt stared at Josh's side. "What are these holes?"

"You're going to be dragging at school," Frank said. "Maybe you should miss tomorrow."

"No, I think I'll be fine. I'm feeling better already."

"It's almost daylight. Okay, you guys take a little snooze. I'll wake you in time for school." Before he walked out of the bathroom, Frank said emphatically, "After school, we're going to talk."

## CHAPTER 20

# TRANSFER STUDENT

Matt had fourth-period study hall in the library. He met Katie at the entrance.

"Are you going to ask Miss Butterfield?"

"Yes, I told you I would," Matt said, tired of her badgering. "I don't know why you don't ask her yourself."

"She doesn't like me," Katie said dejectedly. "You'll have better luck."

Matt refused to argue.

As soon as they stepped into the library, the two friends were hit with its usual strong aroma of peppermint. The librarian kept a large bowl of the candy on her counter, and the scent hung in the air. Matt had actually thought Miss Butterfield wore peppermint perfume when he first met her. He loved the smell, while Katie thought it was obnoxious and overbearing—yet one more thing she disliked about the new librarian.

Miss Butterfield looked up and smiled at Matt. Losing Miss Witherspoon to retirement in Paragon had been very difficult for him, but her replacement exuded cheerfulness. Matt couldn't understand Katie's aversion for the woman.

"Hello, Matthew. I have the book you wanted to read," Miss Butterfield whispered.

This was the opening Matt needed. He walked up to the desk. "That was quick." Matt turned and looked back at Katie, while Miss

Butterfield scanned the book. Katie mouthed, "Ask her," with her words barely audible.

Matt rolled his eyes, then formed a circle with one thumb and forefinger. *Okay.*

"There you go, young man. I hope you enjoy it. It's always been one of my favorites."

Matt leaned forward and rested his elbows on the counter. "You know the other day, when Katie O'Hara had a package left for her in the library—"

"Can you believe that?" The librarian puckered her lips and squinted. "A student receiving packages in the library…with me expected to be the delivery person!"

Matt played along. "I know. What's this world coming to?"

"I'm glad someone understands."

Matt smiled, looking angelic. "Do you have any idea who dropped it off?"

Miss Butterfield leaned closer to Matt. "No. In fact, the library was open and the lights were on that day when I came back from lunch. I still haven't figured out who unlocked the building."

"So you weren't here when the package was delivered."

"It was sitting on my desk when I arrived."

Matt backed away from the counter. "Thank you so much, Miss Butterfield." He held the book up high. "Since it's one of your favorites, I'm really looking forward to reading it," he said, making sure to flatter her.

Miss Butterfield pointed to the bowl of peppermints. Matt reached in and took a piece of candy. "Mmm, thanks."

"You're such a sweet boy. Take a few more for later."

Matt eagerly grabbed a handful of peppermint candies. "You're the greatest!"

The librarian beamed.

Matt turned and walked to the study desk, where Sydney had just joined Katie.

The look on Katie's face was hilarious. "What is it with you and librarians?" she asked with a shrug.

"I don't know what you're talking about," Matt said with a smirk. He knew Miss Butterfield favored him. But there was no way he would admit it to Katie.

"'Have a wonderful day, young man. Take as many peppermints as you like,'" Katie said sarcastically, pointing her nose in the air.

"Shh." The librarian held a finger to her lips.

Sydney snickered. "Matt, you are *so* clueless. It's obvious she likes you."

"You girls are way too sensitive. She's nice to everyone."

"Yeah, she's nice to *every boy*!" Sydney whispered.

Katie poked Matt. "Well, does she know?"

Matt looked up quizzically. "Oh that," he said. "No, she said the package was on her desk when she got back from lunch."

Katie groaned. "There was no postage. It was as if someone just walked in and dropped it off."

Matt had a thought. "Miss Butterfield did say the library was unlocked when she got back from lunch. Maybe whoever unlocked the library placed the package on her desk."

Katie tapped the table lightly. "Then it had to be someone on the staff."

"Yeah," Matt said. "But who on staff would leave you such an odd package?" He looked up at the large clock on the north wall of the library. "I can't sit here and talk. I have to get some work done." He walked over to one of the stacks, looking for information on John Adams for Mr. Hardcastle's class.

In a matter of minutes, Matt pulled out a reference book. Yes, it was exactly what he needed. He rushed into the main corridor, and immediately ran into something…more like someone. A short girl, not anyone he recognized, fell backward, and an armful of books scattered on the floor.

"I'm so sorry," Matt said, picking up a large social studies book.

The girl grabbed the book from him.

Matt had hit her pretty hard. Quite concerned, he asked anxiously, "Are you okay?"

The girl looked up at him and said nothing. Her large black eyes, magnified by the thick lenses of her glasses, exposed a level of vulnerability. After gathering her books, she rose up and scurried out of the library.

Matt looked back at Katie, who shrugged. He decided to follow the girl. He grabbed his backpack and raced out of the library. He found her leaning against the building, crying. "Let me take you to the nurse's office. You're hurt. I knew I hit you pretty hard."

Again she said nothing.

He extended his right hand. "By the way, I'm Matt Monroe."

Katie walked out of the library. The girl took one look at Katie and practically ran down the sidewalk.

Matt gave Katie an odd look. "What's her story?"

"She's a transfer," Katie said. "Her family is from Romania. How weird is that? Apparently, her dad is some kind of scientist."

Sydney joined them. "You should see their house. They live on Park Lane."

"What's her name?" Matt asked.

Katie snickered. "Izadora Vassavich."

"Whoa, that's a tongue twister. I'd hate to write that out every time I had to sign my name," Matt said.

"I call her Frizzy Izzy. Did you see her hair?"

Stunned by her remark, Matt said, "That's pretty rude, even for you."

Katie's face turned red. Matt knew for sure it was from anger, not embarrassment.

"She's not very friendly," Sydney said. "She thinks she's better than everyone."

"How can you say that?" Matt asked, leaning against a hand railing that ran the length of the landing. "You don't even know her. She might just be shy."

Katie laughed. "Did you get a look at those glasses?"

Matt snarled. "What's wrong with you?" He shook his head in disgust. "You wore glasses every bit as thick until just a few weeks ago."

The tension rose rapidly.

"Why do you care?" Katie asked. "The girl's a jerk... Frizzy Izzy."

Matt pushed past them. He couldn't deal with their ignorance.

Izadora got off the school bus and darted home. She quickly climbed the winding staircase to her second-floor bedroom. Chestnut Mountain Academy was her third school in two years. Izadora's horrendous shyness had made the constant changing of schools a traumatic experience for her. It took her a long time to make new friends, and the girls at this school were by far the least friendly she had ever encountered.

As soon as she entered the bedroom, Izadora locked the door. She flopped onto her bed and burst into tears. Shortly, a light tapping sounded on the door. When she didn't answer, the person on the other side jiggled the doorknob. Soon the knocking stopped.

She replayed the incident in the library. The boy who rammed into her appeared to be sincere. But why didn't she answer him? Simple—she was embarrassed by her thick Eastern European accent. Besides, why would a cute boy want to talk to her? She was overweight, and her hair was a mess, a gene she had inherited from her mother's side of the family. *He was just going to tease me.*

Izadora stared into the mirror. Even hidden by glasses, her eyes looked red and swollen from all her tears. She pulled on her scalp. Her hair did its own thing no matter how much she tried to fix it. *Who am I kidding? Even I wouldn't talk to me.*

The tapping on her bedroom door started again. This time she opened the door. Her maternal grandmother stood in the hallway.

Nana looked at her with sad eyes. "How is my little Dorie lamb? Did you have a bad day at school?" she asked in Romanian.

Answering in English, Izadora said, "It was no different from any other day."

This time in broken English, her grandmother said, "You good girl. In time they see this. Come eat. Dinner ready."

Dorie gave her a big hug. "I'll be down. I have to freshen up first."

A few minutes later, Izadora joined her family for dinner. Her mother, father, and little brother sat at the table.

"Where's Nana?" she asked.

Her mother rolled her eyes. "Come on, honey. Isn't that a silly question?"

An extraordinary room sat in the far corner of the basement, a space where Nana spent most of her waking hours. No matter where they lived, Izadora's father made sure his mother-in-law had her special room.

Until a few years ago, Izadora had no idea what happened in that room. It was off-limits to her. On her twelfth birthday, her grandmother revealed the room's purpose. Now Izadora wished she were still clueless.

"Nana wants to talk with you after dinner," her father said.

Izadora almost choked on the small bite of food in her mouth. If anyone in school found out about her grandmother's special room, she would never make a friend. That information would condemn her to a life as an outcast.

*It's always so dark down here*, Izadora thought as she descended the basement steps. The old wood squeaked with each step.

"Is that you, Dorie?"

Dorie laughed to herself. Nana supposedly had a hearing problem. What a joke. She figured her grandmother had the best ears in the family.

"Yes, Nana, it's me."

Dorie saw the familiar flickering of candlelight. She admired her grandmother's dramatic flair. Electric lighting would never do in her special room. Her smile faded as she strolled into the small chamber. Even though she had entered it hundreds of times in many different houses, the place still unsettled her. The walls and ceiling, painted black, exuded a sense of foreboding. An antique round maple table, covered with a purple felt tablecloth, sat in the middle of the mysterious room. A white linen handkerchief hid an object in the center of the table, while a candle flickered on a lonely stand in the far corner. Next to the candle sat a picture of Dorie and her grandmother, taken in Bucharest. Unknown to Dorie, a set of skeleton keys lay hidden behind the photo.

Her grandmother motioned for her to take the only other seat at the table.

"What did you want to see me about, Nana?"

Her grandmother said in Romanian, "*Stai, copil.*"

Dorie did as told and sat down. Nana grabbed Dorie's right hand and stared with sympathetic eyes. Again, speaking in Romanian, she said, "I have noticed you are very unhappy in this new house."

Out of respect, Dorie answered in Romanian. "I'm fine. It'll take a while to adjust." She didn't want to burden her grandmother with her problems.

"Nonsense. There is a reason for your uneasiness."

Dorie bowed her head and moaned. *Not again!*

"Your destiny is upon you. Your purpose in life lies here. It is as though you have come home."

These kinds of talks had been mystifying to her as a young girl, but now they just plain irritated her. Much as she didn't want to upset her grandmother, Nana's constant predictions, which flew way off the mark, irked her. "Nana, you said that when we moved the last time."

Her grandmother raised her right hand. This meant *silence*. "I misread the signs."

When Dorie groaned, her grandmother cast a sneer at her.

"Enough with doubting!" her grandmother said firmly. "You have inherited a very special gift. Your mother only wishes she had this power. It has been passed down in our family for over a thousand years." She reached across the table and grabbed Dorie's hand. "It has now been passed to you!"

"I told you I don't want it!" Dorie shouted in English, pulling away from her grandmother. "Nana, please, I don't want to offend you, but I don't want your magic."

The old woman grabbed her chest. "I know this, and it breaks my heart."

Dorie hadn't meant to upset her grandmother. She got up and tried to hug her, but the old woman pushed her aside.

"Leave me. Let me sit and meditate."

"I don't want to hurt you," Dorie said with her head bowed. "But this is America. Your old-country thinking doesn't fit in here."

"You think you're hurting me? The only person you are hurting is yourself." She stared directly at Dorie with sad eyes. "You will be miserable until you accept your destiny."

## CHAPTER 21

# KINGSTON DRAGON

Matt waited anxiously for his father to get home from work. He sat in the recliner, mindlessly bouncing a tennis ball off the paneled wall.

Josh bounded down the steps into the game room. "Want to play a game of pool?"

Matt jumped out of the recliner. "Sure, rack 'em up." He broke the triangular set-up with a direct hit. Balls scattered over the entire table. The number nine ball fell into the side pocket. "I'm stripes. You're solids."

"Nice break," Josh said.

"Thanks. Where's Mom?" Matt asked as he lined up his next shot.

"Didn't Dad text you? She and Mrs. Roundtree are shopping. Then they're going to dinner. Girls' night out."

Matt snickered. "You've got to hand it to the old man. He had to get Mom out of the house somehow. What better way than a shopping spree?"

A voice yelled from upstairs. "Are you boys home?"

"We're in the game room," Josh hollered back.

Footsteps pounded the wooden stairs. Their father entered the game room, carrying two boxes of pizza, which he placed on a side table. Josh got cold drinks from the fridge.

"You know, we should to this more often," Frank said, preparing to bite into a piece of pepperoni pizza. He nestled into his favorite chair and got right to the point. "So, boys, tell me about last night."

Matt looked at Josh, Josh looked at Matt. Who should start the conversation?

Josh spoke first. "Actually, Dad, I don't know what happened. Like I said, I walked outside to get some air because I couldn't sleep. I don't remember anything till Sport found me in the tree house."

"What about you, Matty? What can you tell me?"

Thankfully, their father had calmed down from the night before, so Matt wasn't keeping anything from him.

"I woke up and Josh was gone. I went out to look for him, but I couldn't find him anywhere. So I walked to the ball field."

Frank raised his eyebrows but said nothing at first. After a pause, he spoke. "So did you find Josh at the playground?"

Josh answered for Matt. "No, he found me in the tree house."

Matt couldn't delay it any longer. "I saw something horrible near the pavilion." He stopped and took a deep breath. "It was a dragon!"

Frank's eyes opened wide and his body stiffened.

Josh grunted, showing his irritation. "Why didn't you tell me?"

"I did." Matt's face filled with compassion. "But you were out of it."

Frank leaned back in his chair. "Let me get this straight. Josh went missing. You went out to find him. Then you walked to the ball field and saw what you think was a dragon."

"It *was* a dragon. It was smaller than the one in Paragon, but it was a dragon...and I think it was carrying Josh."

Frank jumped forward. "What!"

Josh froze, stupefied by Matt's news. "A dragon grabbed me?"

"Mr. Sherman was at the ball field. Ask him," Matt said defensively. "He shot at the dragon as it flew away. He said it was carrying a calf."

Matt walked over to Josh and told him to lift his shirt. He showed their dad the small, circular welts on his brother's right side. "I don't think the dragon was carrying a calf at all. I think it was carrying

Josh! Some of the buckshot hit right here," he said, pointing to the tiny pockmarks. "I think Mr. Sherman saved Josh's life when he hit the dragon with the shotgun blast."

Frank peered at Josh's wound. "They do look like pellet marks."

Matt turned to Josh. "I'm pretty sure it was the dragon that cut your left side. Your clothes were shredded. It must have grabbed you in the ball field. You probably climbed into the tree house to hide after it dropped you."

Josh turned pale. "I don't remember anything."

"Let's keep this from your mother for the time being," Frank said, rubbing his chin nervously. "I have to talk to King Darius. I hope my contact works out."

"Dad, we know someone who can communicate with Paragon," Josh said, reaching for another piece of pizza.

Frank looked puzzled. "Who?"

"Grandma Elsa," Josh said.

"Mrs. Worthington?"

Matt chuckled. "She's sweet on Pappy Jack."

"Grandma told us she meets with him regularly," Josh said. "Pappy Jack told her about our trip to Paragon. I bet she can get a message to the king through him."

Frank burst into laughter. "That old dog! He never ceases to amaze me."

"Josh, are you awake?" Matt whispered.

"I am now."

"I didn't mean to wake you."

"I'm ragging you. I can't sleep either."

Matt sat up in bed. "Okay if I turn on the light?" Since Josh didn't answer, Matt took that as a yes. Even though it was only a forty-watt bulb, the lamp lit up the room. "Do you think we'll be going back to Paragon?"

Josh leaned over to face Matt. "Who knows? But the fact that a dragon is loose in Kingston can't be kept a secret for very long."

"Yeah, I wonder if Mr. Sherman said anything to the police," Matt said. "I know he's upset about losing those cattle."

"I don't think we have to worry about him."

"Why?"

"Picture this. He goes to the police station and tells them a dragon is roaming around Kingston. The cops grab him and force him into an ambulance, headed to the nearest loony bin."

Matt snickered. "I can just see it now. He's carried to the ambulance, kicking and screaming."

Josh pounded his mattress. "Can you imagine the words coming out of his mouth? Get your effin' hands off me, you son-of-a-b—"

Both laughed hysterically. Matt picked up his pillow and tossed it. He hit Josh in the head with a perfect shot. Next thing, both boys rolled around on the floor, wrestling.

There was a knock at the door. "What's going on in there?" their mother asked.

"Sorry, Mom," Josh called. "We're just talking."

"You better knock it off and get some sleep. It's late."

"Okay," Matt answered, but he couldn't stop snickering. Visions of Mr. Sherman kicking and screaming kept him wide awake. The last time he checked his phone, it was 3:15 a.m.

## CHAPTER 22

# RECONCILIATION

Matt slowly stepped out of the car in the school parking lot. It would take everything he had to stay awake, especially in Mr. Werner's class.

Zach slammed the back door. "That was the quietest ride I've ever had to school."

"What do you mean?" Matt asked innocently, rubbing his temple. His headache had returned.

"You guys didn't say a word. Not one word. What's wrong?"

Josh looked over at Matt. He had a look of 'don't you say anything' in his eyes, so Matt came up with a story. "I had a really bad dream last night. I woke Josh and we both got practically no sleep. I guess we're just tired."

Matt sighed in relief when Zach quickly changed the subject. "I heard you met Katie's new nemesis."

"Who's that?" Matt asked.

"The girl from Romania."

Matt had wondered how she was doing. She looked so out of place at the academy. "Yeah, I feel bad for her. She's a new kid, and from a foreign country to boot. That has to suck."

"No worries," Zach said. "She's one of us."

"How so?"

"She's a nerd. I talked with her the other day. She's way cool." His face brightened, and a small smile played across his lips. "And her accent is awesome."

Matt had never seen his friend so excited about a girl. He grinned at Josh and punched Zach lightly on the arm. "Could this be your first girl—"

Zach stopped Matt in midsentence. "Look at Rico, staring us down."

Before he could answer, Matt heard a voice that caused chills to run down his spine.

"Morning, Josh," Mitzi Martel said.

Josh ignored her and ran ahead to catch up with Katie, who waited for him farther up the hall.

Mitzi stamped her foot petulantly. "One of these days I'm going to ignore him. We'll see how he likes it." She sauntered over to Matt. "You tell your brother he better call me!"

No sooner had Katie gotten the locker door open than it slammed shut.

Mitzi Martel and her posse stood directly behind her. Mitzie held her right hand securely on the locker's door. "I guess you didn't hear me the first time," she said spitefully. "Stay away from Josh!"

"Or what?" Katie asked, ready for a fight.

Mitzi shoved her into the locker.

"Can't you see? He only feels sorry for you," Mitzi said with contempt.

Brittany giggled, obviously enjoying Katie's predicament, while Dani, who stood watch in the hall, looked around nervously. "Let's get out of here," Dani pleaded.

Mitzi grabbed Katie even tighter. "You're just not his type," she said, flaring her nostrils. "First of all—you're not attractive—at all."

Caught off guard, Katie felt tears forming in her eyes. She didn't want the obnoxious cheerleader to see her cry, so she pushed her way past Mitzi and ran down the hall. She turned the corner and jumped into the first unlocked room. It was the girls' lavatory. Katie ran into an open stall just as tears started to flow. She locked the door behind her and wept loudly. *Is Mitzi right? Does Josh just feel sorry for me?*

In just a few seconds, the door to the bathroom flew open. Katie heard voices. It was Mitzi and her crew. She quickly grabbed some toilet tissue and covered her nose and mouth, trying to muffle her sobbing.

Mitzi said with amusement, "I guess I showed her."

Katie looked through the crack between the stall doors and watched the cheerleaders primping in the mirror.

Brittany stood beside Mitzi, applying lip gloss. "I don't think she'll want to mess with you again."

Mitzi cocked her head to the side. "I wish Josh wouldn't lower himself to associate with such losers."

Dani stood back. "What you said to her was mean!" Her voice trembled with anger.

Mitzi contorted her face with a 'how could you question me' glare. "What did you say?"

"You heard me," Dani said. "Are you that insecure, that you'd hurt a little girl?"

Katie leaned forward in the stall. *This is getting good.*

Mitzi stepped into Dani's space. "You'd better watch yourself."

"I don't know why I ever thought you could be my friend. You're everything I loathe. You're nothing but a bully." Dani turned and walked toward the door.

Mitzi grabbed Dani's arm. "You walk out that door and our friendship is over."

Brittany stood still as a statue, nervously cracking her wad of gum. She watched her friends spar back and forth.

Dani pursed her lips. "We never were friends."

"If you walk out now, you're dead to me."

Dani grabbed the door handle and turned back. "You want to know why Josh doesn't give you the time of day? Because you're nothing but a self-absorbed brat!" She stormed out of the bathroom.

Katie snickered lightly, but quickly covered her mouth so her presence wouldn't be discovered.

Mitzi's face flushed, red with rage. "I'm so mad I could spit."

"Don't waste your time on her," Brittany said. "She never really was one of us. We're so much better than her."

"You are *so* right. Wait till cheerleading practice. I'll make her pay." The two girls opened the door and strutted out of the bathroom.

Katie slowly stepped out of the bathroom stall, looking around to make sure the coast was clear. She walked to the sink and peered into the mirror. Her puffy red eyes stared back at her.

The door to another stall opened. Out walked Izadora Vassavich. "Are you okay?"

Katie's humiliation was complete. "Leave me alone," she said angrily, in no mood to deal with anyone, let alone the transfer student.

After last bell, Josh spied Katie standing in the back hall. "Where's Sport?" he asked.

Katie grunted. "He and Zach are working in the library, earning brownie points with Miss Butterfield. It's not like they need them."

"That's right. I forgot…Mrs. Roundtree's picking them up later."

Chad joined them. "Hey guys, did you hear what happened between the two princesses?"

"No, what's up?" Josh asked. He could tell by the excitement in Chad's voice that his friend couldn't wait to give him the scoop.

Chad snickered. "You didn't hear about the big blowup between Mitzi and Dani? The whole school's talking about it."

Katie nonchalantly said, "Mitzi picked on me, and Dani came to my defense."

"Oh, that must have been priceless," Josh said, sorry he had missed the confrontation.

Katie grinned. "It was... I thought she was going to deck Dani."

"Where did this happen?" Chad asked.

Katie blushed. "In the girl's bathroom."

Just then Dani Halverson passed by. Josh called out to her, but she walked away. In fact, it looked like she actually sped up her pace. "Dani," he called out again.

Josh caught up with her as she stepped out of the building onto the cement plaza near the tennis courts. "Dani, I want to talk with you." He stepped in front of her. She had no choice but to stop. "I want to thank you for standing up for Katie."

Dani looked up. Josh noticed her red eyes. He grabbed her right arm. "What's wrong?"

She pulled away. "Like you care!"

Josh got a sick feeling in his stomach. "I know I've been a jerk to you lately. I just can't stand the idea you joined up with those two."

"I quit the squad. Are you happy? I only tried to be friends with Mitzi because we were both cheerleaders. But today she stepped over the line. What she said to Katie was totally wrong."

Josh grabbed Dani's hand. She pushed him away again and raced toward the student parking lot.

Josh ran up to her. "I'm sorry," he said, his voice cracking.

Dani turned toward Josh. "We used to be good friends. What happened to us?"

"You changed. Once you became a cheerleader, you seemed to—"

"I only joined the squad because I thought..." Dani looked down. When she looked up, tears ran down her cheeks. "I thought you'd like me more."

"What? Why would you think that?"

Dani stared defiantly at Josh. She said caustically, "You think Mitzi is full of herself? When you led the swim team to the regional championship last year, you were too big to spend time with me anymore.

So I thought if I was a cheerleader you'd pay attention to me. Now I don't even care."

Josh scrunched his forehead.

Dani stepped closer to him. "Don't act so clueless. You're just as full of yourself as Mitzi… Maybe you two are a good match."

Josh's face flushed with embarrassment. "Touché."

Dani smiled smugly, pleased with herself.

Josh hadn't realized how much he had hurt Dani, so he decided to give in and start over. He extended his right hand. "Hi, my name is Josh Monroe." He hoped she would play along.

Dani raised her eyebrows, and Josh watched the anger drain from her beautiful green eyes.

She grabbed Josh's right hand. "I'm Dani Halverson. It's nice to meet you."

"Well, Dani Halverson, I think we should get to know each other a little better and see where it goes."

Dani's face appeared wary, but Josh did not wait for a response. He quickly leaned forward and gave her a full hug.

Dani stuttered, "I-I've—"

"Do you want to go out sometime?" Josh blurted out. "I've missed you," he whispered in her ear.

A shrill scream echoed across the quad. Mitzi and Brittany stood only thirty feet away. Both girls had their hands on their hips, with Mitzi's face drawn. Her eyes resembled flaming embers.

Josh spied the cheerleaders and threw them a kiss. He grabbed Dani's right hand. "Do you need a ride home?"

"No… I drove. But I'll walk with you."

Mitzi called out, "Where do you think you're going?" She ran toward them, but Josh and Dani crossed the small roadway into the student parking lot. Oncoming buses blocked Mitzi's path. Fate had intervened.

"No!" Mitzi screamed. "This can't happen." The realization of Josh with Dani crushed Mitzi. She always got her way—but not this time.

Brittany glared. "How dare she."

Mitzi turned toward her friend and burst into tears. She fell into Brittany's arms, totally devastated by Josh's rejection.

Brittany patted Mitzi's back. "He doesn't deserve you. When he realizes what a loser Dani is, he'll come crawling back to you."

Mitzi composed herself. In a determined voice, she said, "I will never shed another tear over that boy…ever again."

## CHAPTER 23

# MISUNDERSTANDING…OR NOT?

Thick fingers of low-lying fog floated toward Matt. Curiosity urged him to walk forward, but what lay ahead? He couldn't see a thing through the odorless vapor. As if on command, the mist lifted and silhouettes formed; trees and shrubs materialized. The outline of a building soon came into view—the Payne mansion. As Matt approached, he observed two lifeless bodies sprawled on the porch near the front door. *Nathaniel and Annabelle!* The children wore old-fashioned nightshirts covered in blood. Their ghost-white skin and lifeless eyes overwhelmed Matt. *They're dead… He killed them.*

In a split second, the children stood next to him on the lawn. Startled, Matt struggled for breath.

Nathaniel, who had a zombie-like appearance reached out and grabbed Matt's arm. "You have to get out of here. You are in grave danger." He turned and peered at the front door, and then back to Matt. "Save your brother."

"But you're bleeding badly. You need help."

"It's too late for us," Annabelle said in a whisper. "Save your brother."

The little girl shoved Matt. Surprised by her strength, he lost his balance and fell backward. He landed on his behind and found himself sitting on his bed, drenched in sweat. Matt slammed a fist into his pillow in frustration. *Why do I keep dreaming about those kids?*

Katie hummed a tune she couldn't get out of her head as she worked on an assignment in the basement of the library. She loved this section of the building because it contained so many fabulous books. It had been revealed to her by Dr. Monroe that Dr. Agregeous Payne donated the many ancient texts to the school.

Today she worked diligently on a term paper about the Roman Republic for Latin class. Katie walked over to one of the glass-fronted bookshelves and immediately found the manuscript she needed. She pulled on the handle, but it did not budge. *When will I remember that they're locked?*

She headed to the main floor of the library to get Miss Butterfield, who had the key to open the case. Just thinking about it caused her stomach to ache. Miss Witherspoon had been so helpful and encouraging, whereas this new librarian seemed to go out of her way to make Katie's day miserable.

As Katie neared the staircase, she noticed the blond librarian turn the corner and walk down the aisle near the far wall of the basement. *Good*, Katie thought. *Since she's already here, she won't be so bothered to help me.* Mysteriously, a blue light flashed across the ceiling tile, and a sound of buzzing bees filled the room. Katie rushed to the aisle, but when she looked down the row of books, no one was there.

Katie shivered. "I think it's time to take a break," she said to herself as she picked up her books. Katie shoved them into her backpack, and then hiked up the marble staircase to the main floor.

Matt sat at their usual table. He spied Katie as she entered the main floor of the library.

Katie stared at the front desk and screamed…loudly.

Matt jumped. *What the heck?!*

"Katie O'Hara. I will not tolerate that kind of behavior in my library. Do you understand?" Miss Butterfield stood at the main desk with a sour expression.

Katie nodded meekly. "Sorry." With a puzzled look on her face and flushed cheeks, she plopped down into the chair next to Matt.

He looked up. "What's wrong? You look weirded out."

"You're going to think I'm crazy, but—"

Just then, the sound of a heavy book hit the desk and echoed through the library. Zach stood there, glaring at Katie.

He quickly leaned over and said in a loud whisper, "Why do you have to be so mean?"

Katie ignored him, but Zach poked her.

"What's your problem?" she asked, hitting his hand away.

Zach sat down beside her. "I'll tell you what my problem is—you! I don't care what you say to me or how you treat me. But when you start hurting people I care about, that's stepping over the line."

The conversation had escalated into a shouting match. Matt looked over toward the counter to check on Miss Butterfield. Thankfully, she was no longer there, because Zach's voice boomed across the library.

Katie snarled. "Spit it out. I don't know what you're talking about."

Zach slammed his fist on the desk. "If you ever talk to Dorie like that again, we're finished. Do you hear me?"

Matt scanned the room. Practically everyone was staring at them.

Katie pouted. "Did your precious Frizzy Izzy get upset again?"

"Quit calling her that! Her name is Dorie!" Zach stormed out of the library in a huff.

Matt rubbed his forehead. "What did you say to her this time?"

Katie shrugged. "Nothing. I can't help it if that girl's thin-skinned."

Matt didn't wait for an explanation. He stood up and dashed out of the library. He found Zach just outside, pacing back and forth. Matt couldn't remember ever seeing his friend so angry. "Look, I know Katie can be insensitive—"

Zach poked him in the chest. "You know I don't care what she says about me. But I'm not going to sit back and let her pick on Dorie."

Matt got a nasty feeling in the pit of his stomach. "What did she do now?"

Zach stood motionless, breathing deeply. Finally he said, "The other day, Dorie was in the girls' bathroom. Someone ran in and took the stall beside her. The girl was crying. Then the three witches walked into the bathroom. Dorie said the cheerleaders were poking fun at Katie and laughing about something they did to her in the hall. After the girls left, Dorie was shocked when she saw it was Katie who sat in the stall next to her."

Matt got impatient. "But why are *you* mad at Katie?"

Zach slapped the wall. "Because Dorie walked out of the stall and tried to comfort her. What do you think *our* friend did? Katie told her she didn't want her help and called her a loser."

"Are you sure?"

Zach started down the sidewalk. "I knew you'd take her side. You always defend her."

He sped toward Franklin Hall, leaving Matt perplexed.

Matt's mind twisted in knots. Surely Katie wouldn't be so cruel as to call Dorie a loser to her face, especially after what the cheerleaders had put her through.

Rico Steel appeared out of nowhere. "Friend problems?"

In no mood to hear what Rico had to say, Matt waved him off. "It's none of your business."

"I'm just saying... You give your friends way too much credit."

"Get lost," Matt said angrily. "Like I said, it's none of your business."

Rico shrugged his shoulders. "People may not be who you think they are," he said as he strolled away.

Matt bit his lower lip.

The bell rang. Katie rushed out of the library. "Good, you're still here. Let's go to lunch. I want to tell you about a weird thing that happened downstairs in the library."

"Wait a minute," Matt said, astounded by her lack of empathy. "Don't you see how mad Zach is at you?"

Katie chuckled, which irritated Matt even more. "He'll get over it. I can't help it if his new girlfriend is a baby."

"A baby! She wasn't the one crying in the girls' bathroom."

Katie's eyes squinted. "Who told you that?"

"That's not important. How could you be so mean?"

"I knew she couldn't keep her big mouth shut," Katie said.

Katie had been one of his closest friends since he could remember, but this thing she had against the new student from Romania was ridiculous.

He threw his hands in the air. "I give up. What happened to the Katie I used to know? I don't like this new Katie at all."

She stepped closer to Matt. Defiantly, Katie asked, "What are you talking about?"

Thoroughly angry by this time, Matt poked her shoulder. "You don't realize how cruel you've become! God, you're acting just like Mitzi."

Katie's face flushed, but before she could speak, Matt said nastily, "I don't want to hear another word."

Katie's eyes bugged out and her flush deepened. "Fine with me, Mr. High-and-Mighty!"

Matt shoved his books into his locker and slammed the door.

Chad stopped at Matt's locker. "Somebody's ticked off," he said, placing his hand on Matt's shoulder.

"It's just one of those days, if you know what I mean."

"Let's get something to eat. It always calms me down."

"No, you go ahead," Matt said. "I have something to do." On top of it all, he had to attend a counseling session for his panic attacks.

Matt turned the corner and walked right into Rico Steel. He jumped back, bracing for a punch.

"I'm sorry," Rico said. He looked Matt right in the eyes. "My fault. No big deal." The bully walked away without any retaliation.

*What gives?* Matt thought as he climbed the steps to the second floor of Franklin Hall.

He met Mr. Hardcastle at the top of the stairs. *Just great.* Matt prepared for a tongue-lashing, but the stern teacher smiled. "Good afternoon, Matthew. How are you today?"

Caught off-guard, Matt sensed no trace of meanness in the man's voice. The history teacher sounded quite sincere. Matt said with a stutter, "I-I'm fine, sir."

"How's your essay on Mr. Adams coming along?"

Matt stood motionless, dumbfounded by the situation. "It's going well," he said finally, when he realized the teacher waited for a response.

Mr. Hardcastle patted him on the shoulder. "I'm looking forward to reading it." The teacher smiled warmly and descended the stairs, while Matt leaned against the wall, totally confused.

## CHAPTER 24

# REALITY OR FANTASY

Early for his counseling session, Matt had a lot to get off his chest. He looked through the small pane of glass on the side of the door. Dr. Grant sat at his desk, eating his lunch. *Good, he's here.* Matt tapped on the door.

"Enter," a voice inside called out.

Matt slowly eased the door open. "I hope I'm not disturbing you. I know I'm early, but I have some extra time."

Dr. Grant wiped his mouth with a napkin and took a quick sip of coffee. "Pull up a chair. I'm just finishing up my lunch."

Matt quickly sat opposite the school psychologist.

Dr. Grant offered Matt some grapes, which he accepted. "So, Matt, what's up? You seem on edge."

"I don't know where to start." Matt leaned on the desk and sighed. "Is everyone a jerk?"

The psychologist raised his eyebrows. "Evidently someone's disappointed you."

"I just don't understand people. Why do they have to pick on each other? It's so stupid."

Dr. Grant leaned forward. "Human nature can be offensive, that's for sure. Still—"

Before the psychologist could continue, Matt interrupted. "What causes a person who's been picked on all her life to pick on someone else?"

Dr. Grant cleared his throat. "Sometimes people with low self-esteem pick on others to make themselves feel good...feel superior." He sipped his coffee. "May I ask to whom you're referring?"

Matt shook his head. "Nah, it's not important. I guess what you said makes sense. But I wish my friend would grow up."

Dr. Grant stood and walked to his file cabinet. "I don't want to rain on your parade, but some people never grow up." He opened the middle drawer and pulled out a file. "So other than your friend disappointing you, has anything else of interest happened to you?" He opened the file.

Matt saw the name on the file, written in red ink: MATT MONROE. "Where do I start?" he said disgustedly.

The psychologist raised his eyebrows. "At the beginning," he said. "I always find it's best to start there."

Matt rubbed his eyes and groaned. "I think I'm going crazy. Last Saturday I took a bike ride to the old Payne mansion. Two kids were sitting on the porch. They said they lived there. Can you believe that? I actually went inside the house with them. It was clean as a whistle. There was new furniture in the parlor."

"What's so strange about that?"

"Wait... I'm not finished," Matt said. His face flushed. "Later that night, my dad, Josh, and I went back to the house. The house was rundown. It was empty with no signs anyone lived there."

Dr. Grant leaned close and said in a whisper, "I think it's that house."

"What?"

"It seems that all your dreams take place at or near that house. Seeing children no one else can see is not normal, Matt. Your anxiety is causing you to hallucinate."

Matt jumped up. "I *did* see them. It wasn't a hallucination."

"Calm down," the psychologist said. "We don't fully understand the workings of the conscious mind. How can any of us be sure of what's real and what's fantasy?"

Matt took a step back.

Dr. Grant smiled sympathetically at Matt. "I feel that house is a big part of your anxiety. And that anxiety is causing you to see things…real or unreal."

Matt gulped. *If he only knew.*

"Think about it. It appears your visits to that house trigger your nightmares. My advice is to stay away from that place…at least for now." Dr. Grant stood and walked Matt to his office door. "Then let's see if the dreams go away completely."

*Maybe Dr. Grant is right*, he pondered as the door closed behind him.

As Matt turned the corner, he heard the echo of a door slamming. "Come here!" Dr. Grant commanded.

Matt assumed the teacher had called to him, so he walked back. Nathaniel Parker, of all people, stood at the far end of the hall. Dr. Grant made a dash toward the boy, who quickly descended the steps.

The detective inside him pushed Matt to follow them. Just as he exited the stairwell, Matt saw the counselor duck outside Franklin Hall and run toward the library, with Nathaniel far ahead of him. Matt followed closely behind.

When he entered the library, Matt lost sight of them. Luckily Zach stood at the counter, checking out a book.

"Did you see Dr. Grant?" Matt asked.

"He went downstairs," Zach said.

Matt hurried down the steps. *I knew I wasn't hallucinating*, he thought excitedly. *But what is Nathaniel doing here?* The basement appeared empty, but a shadow soon showed on the wall. Matt was sure they had run down the far aisle.

"Get away from me," Nathaniel hollered.

Matt snuck over and took a quick look. Sure enough, Dr. Grant stood next to the boy. He had Nathaniel securely by the arm.

The psychologist turned around and faced Matt. There was a flash of bright blue light, accompanied by a low buzzing resonance. Dr. Grant and Nathaniel vanished, while Matt staggered and fell to the floor.

Matt opened his eyes slowly. His head ached, and he rubbed a large bump on his forehead. Matt held onto the banister as he shakily climbed the marble stairs. He entered the main floor of the library and found no one there. *Where is everyone?*

Matt spied Miss Butterfield humming to herself.

"Good morning, Matthew," the librarian said. "I didn't see you come in."

*Good morning?* a bewildered Matt asked himself. *It's late afternoon!*

"You look disheveled. Are you okay?"

"What day is it?" Matt shook his head as if to clear his confusion.

Miss Butterfield smiled. "I heard you were a kidder. Why, it's Wednesday, you silly boy."

The lights dimmed and the room began to spin. Matt slumped over, then someone grabbed his right arm. It was Miss Butterfield.

"Are you all right?" she asked.

He blushed. "Yes, I'm sorry. I didn't sleep well last night. Sorry to bother you."

"No bother." She walked Matt over to a large study desk. "Sit here. I'll get you some juice."

*What's happening to me?* He reached for his chest and felt the small amulet given to him by Madame Violet.

Soon the library bustled with students.

"There you are!" a voice behind him called. It was Katie. Unbelievably, Dorie and Zach stood next to her. They all seemed perfectly happy with each other.

"Hi," Matt said, totally bewildered.

"Josh said your dad dropped you off today… Something about an early meeting with Dr. Grant. But no one's seen you. Where've you been?"

Matt sipped his orange juice. *I think I'm losing my mind.*

# CHAPTER 25

# BIG ANNOUNCEMENT

Sitting in Mr. Werner's class, Matt, of course, daydreamed. His head ached, and a bout of nausea overtook him. *Am I getting sick?* He touched his forehead—no fever. He fought to stay awake and positioned his fists under his chin, with his elbows firmly locked together on the desktop to keep from falling forward. It was to no avail; he drifted off anyway.

"I graded your essays," Mr. Werner suddenly barked out.

The sudden rise in the teacher's voice caused Matt to jump. He actually moaned slightly as he regained full consciousness. He wiped the drool from his lower lip and looked around. Thankfully, no one had seemed to notice.

"I read your essays on Act I of the play," the teacher said in a somewhat amused tone. He leaned against the blackboard. "Some were good, others were… How shall I put it?" He grunted. "Not so good. Only one was excellent." He walked over to his desk and held up a single essay. "But one in particular was quite medicinal."

Katie raised her hand. Mr. Werner acknowledged her. She asked, "What do you mean, sir?"

"About the paper I hold in my hand?"

"What do you mean, it was medicinal?"

Mr. Werner chuckled. "Odd that you should ask. You know I've had trouble falling asleep at night."

Matt snorted. *Join the club. I know how that feels.*

Mr. Werner leaned on his desk. "But thanks to you, Miss O'Hara, I've found a cure for my insomnia."

He waved Katie's paper back and forth.

The room erupted into laughter. Matt looked over at Katie. She sat expressionless, apparently in shock.

Mr. Werner posed this explanation. "I told you to write a thousand-word essay, not *Gone with the Wind*. You made a wonderful argument in the first page of your paper. But before I could finish your *long…long…long* dissertation, thankfully I fell asleep." He closed his eyes and pretended to nod off.

Everyone whooped uncontrollably. Even Katie had a grin on her face.

"Brevity, Miss O'Hara. Learn to keep it short and simple," the teacher stated.

"Who wrote the excellent essay?" Katie's curiosity had gotten the best of her.

Mr. Werner smirked. His eyebrows rose as he walked toward the back of the classroom. "I must say I was surprised by this student's efforts. Congratulations, Mr. Monroe. Excellent work." He dropped the paper on Matt's desk.

In red ink, a large A+ had been marked on the essay. Mr. Werner leaned down and whispered, "I can't imagine the work you are capable of…if you could stay awake in my class."

Matt looked up sheepishly. The teacher grinned from ear to ear and actually winked.

In a blur, Matt found himself at lunch. He sat with his friends, unsure of himself. *Is this a dream or is it real?*

Everything appeared to be normal—Chad as entertaining as ever, and Bill obsessed with something trivial. At the table to his left, Josh laughed heartily, but Matt noticed a faraway look in his brother's eyes that belied his laughter. Josh's face seemed drawn and his eyes looked tired.

Matt got up and walked over to his brother. "Are you okay?"

"Yeah, why wouldn't I be?" Josh said with disdain.

Matt knew a dodge when he heard one, so he headed back to his table, figuring he'd wait till they got home to question his brother.

Matt left lunch early for his counseling session. He reluctantly trekked to Dr. Grant's office. Oh, how he didn't want to go to that meeting. Matt looked inside the room through the small window on the side of the door. The school psychologist sat at his desk. It looked like he had just finished his lunch. Matt knocked lightly.

"Enter," a voice called out.

"It's me." Matt ambled into the small room.

Dr. Grant looked over his reading glasses. "You're early." Matt noted a hint of concern in the man's voice.

The psychologist motioned toward the chair in front of his desk. "Sit, Matt." He tossed a crumpled brown paper bag into the nearby trash can. It landed dead center in the small container.

"Two points!" Matt shouted.

Dr. Grant looked puzzled.

"You know, basketball? You just made a basket."

Dr. Grant let Matt's joke pass without comment. He leaned back and placed both hands behind his head, locked together. "Have you had any more dreams?"

"No, sir. Things seem to have calmed down," Matt said, covering up the truth. He didn't feel comfortable telling the psychologist anything else, at least not at this time, since he had no plans to stop going to the Payne estate.

Dr. Grant leaned forward. "You wouldn't be holding out on me now, would you?" he asked with a slight snarl. "You know everything you tell me is confidential."

Matt detected an air of frustration in the man's voice. "I must be healing. I'm sleeping straight through the night. You said the nightmares would go away when my mind heals from the trauma."

"Yes, that's true. Have you been feeling better?"

Out of habit when nervous, Matt reached inside his shirt and grabbed hold of the amulet from Paragon.

"What's that?"

Matt anxiously rubbed the exotic souvenir. "Just something I got in Paragon." *Did I just say Paragon?* This realization caused Matt to squirm.

"Paragon?"

"It's a small island off Mexico." Proud of his quick thinking, Matt opened the top two buttons on his shirt and pulled the amulet out into full view.

"I've never heard of Paragon, but that shell is beautiful. I don't think I've ever seen anything like it," Dr. Grant said, pulling the amulet closer to him.

A strange feeling came over Matt, an urgent sense of alarm. He jumped up and made an excuse to leave. "I forgot… I have to go to my locker before my next class. I need to get a book." His breathing, quick and shallow, caused him to feel faint.

Dr. Grant grabbed Matt's arm. "Are you sure you're okay?" he asked with genuine concern. "Are you having another panic attack?"

Matt pulled free of the counselor. "No," he said defensively, as he scurried out of the room. He rounded the corner and leaned against the wall, struggling to make sense of the last twenty-four hours. *What's real: this meeting or the one I had earlier?*

A slammed door woke Matt from his funk. He peeked around the corner. Nathaniel Parker stood near the stairwell!

Dr. Grant opened his door and jumped into the hall. "Wait, I want to talk with you," the psychologist said to Nathaniel.

Nathaniel ran. Dr. Grant followed, dashing toward the stairwell. They took the steps down to the main floor of the school.

Matt freaked—the scene mirrored what he had observed earlier. He scooted down the stairs and raced toward the library. Matt knew instinctively where they had gone, so he entered the library and headed for the basement.

Matt turned the corner and ran head-on into Dr. Grant.

"That must have been a quick trip to your locker."

Matt fumbled for an answer. "I'm having a strange day. The book was actually in my backpack after all."

"Are you *sure* you're okay?" Dr. Grant asked once more. "You look frazzled."

Matt just wanted to get out of there.

"I want to show you something." The counselor led Matt down the aisle. "Did you ever hear of the Parker family?"

"No, who are they?" he asked, trying to hide his shock at the question.

"At the turn of the twentieth century, two children were murdered in Kingston. They lived in the Payne mansion. It was the big scandal of its day."

Matt reacted indifferently. He had become a pro at hiding his true emotions.

The teacher tapped the glass in front of him. "Inside are microfilm reels of the old newspaper clippings of the crime. If you ever want to look at them, let me know. They never did find the murderer."

Matt entered the library and spotted Katie at their usual table, but the girl who sat beside her flabbergasted him—Izadora Vassavich! Katie actually had her left arm draped around Dorie.

Matt plopped down in the open seat across from Katie. "Hi," he said. He looked at Katie, then back to Dorie. Both smiled, apparently quite comfortable with each other. *Am I in the twilight zone?*

"Dorie, can you get me that reference book I mentioned earlier?" Katie asked.

"Sure." Dorie jumped up and walked across the library to fetch the book.

"Dorie needed help with American History," Katie said quickly. "So I volunteered to help her out."

Matt raised his eyebrows.

Katie sighed. "You were right. She's really nice…and smart."

Unexpectedly, a large book slammed down on the desk. It was Zach. In a disgusted tone, he said, "Mr. Hardcastle's a total idiot."

A loud *Shh* came from the direction of Miss Butterfield.

Dorie returned to the table and slyly passed Matt a note. Zach and Katie were busy discussing Mr. Hardcastle and missed the handoff.

Matt opened the small piece of paper under the table. He quickly scanned the message, and then crumpled the note. "Dorie, can you help me find some information for my science project?" he asked.

Dorie turned toward Katie. "Would that be okay?"

"Your head has to be ready to explode," Katie said. "Yeah, take a break."

Matt and Dorie strolled to a remote part of the library, where they wouldn't be seen by their friends. They stepped inside an unoccupied study room. Matt closed the door. "What did you mean in your note?" he asked.

Dorie's lips trembled. "I haven't told anyone else about this. Not even Zach."

"Okay, I'll bite," he said.

She motioned for Matt to sit and took the seat opposite him. "My grandmother has a special gift. I didn't say anything about it before because I've had enough trouble at this school." She looked down as if embarrassed. "I have the same gift."

"Spill. So what's your gift?"

Dorie cringed and leaned back in her chair. "I'm descended from a tribe of Romanian gypsies." She stopped and took a deep breath.

"No big deal," he said, trying to allay her fears.

"But gypsies are not welcome in most social circles."

To Matt, it sounded like she already regretted having mentioned it. "Look, Dorie, I'm on your side. If you knew the truth about my family, you wouldn't be so nervous. I'm sure my family could out-weird yours any day."

"I'm telling you this because…because you're in great danger."

Matt shivered. *Where is this going?* He offered her a fake smile.

After a long pause, she said, "I need a piece of your clothing to help you." Despite the cool temperature in the room, her forehead beaded with sweat.

"That's it? Heck, that doesn't even record a minor blip on my family's weirdness chart."

Dorie blurted out, "I read crystals…well, actually, a crystal ball. I see things inside a crystal ball." She dropped her head and buried her face in her hands.

"Is that even possible?" Matt exclaimed, taken aback.

When Dorie looked up, Matt saw the look of fear in her eyes. He quickly attempted to calm her. "Don't worry…I think it's cool. I just didn't know anyone could actually do it."

"You don't find this weird?"

"Interesting, but not weird." The girl's story fascinated him.

Dorie sat expressionless for a moment, and then she sighed deeply. "I know everyone thinks gypsies are charlatans at county fairs who rip people off. Those people *are* frauds. They're probably not even real gypsies."

She grabbed Matt's hand. "There truly are very few people who can actually see something in the crystal. I just happen to be one of the *lucky ones*!"

Matt detected her sarcasm. *I do like this girl.*

"You'll know when a gypsy is the real thing," Dorie said. "Because she won't charge you for her gift."

The capitalist side of Matt showed through. "If you can't charge, what good is it?"

"You can't charge… But you can always accept a donation." Dorie said with a sly grin.

Matt chuckled at her response, then opened his backpack and pulled out a baseball cap. "Will this do?"

"That's perfect." Dorie jumped up and pointed toward the glass panel in the door. "Something's going on."

Students packed the library. Matt opened the door, and the two waded through the large crowd to reach Katie and Zach.

"What's up?" Matt asked, when he reached his friends.

Katie rolled her eyes. "Her royal highness, Princess Mitzi, has an announcement to make." Matt looked toward the checkout counter, and sure enough, there stood the obnoxious cheerleader and her posse, huddled together.

"Attention, everyone," the librarian announced.

Dorie said, "Are you sure that's Miss Butterfield and not a clone?"

Miss Butterfield raised her voice. "Can I have your attention, please? Mitzi has some great news to share with you."

Katie moaned audibly. "I think I'm going to be sick."

The smug cheerleader walked to the front counter and smirked.

Looking around the room, Matt couldn't believe how many students seemed to be taken in by the girl.

"This is so exciting," Mitzi said with a self-satisfied giggle. "We have a venue for our Halloween dance. An *amazing* venue, I should say. Dr. Monroe has given us permission to hold our dance at the Payne estate!" She grabbed Miss Butterfield, and together they jumped up and down.

A loud roar rose up, causing the windows to rattle. Katie gagged. "I'm going to throw up. Just look at Miss Butterfield. It's sickening."

Dorie leaned closer to Katie. "If that were us making this racket, we'd be sitting in the office in two seconds. But her girls can do anything."

Matt noticed Dani Halverson, sitting alone at a far table. He walked over. "You're not joining the celebration?"

She shrugged. "They're fools. Between you and me, it was Josh who convinced your dad to let us hold the dance there."

Matt sat down at the table. "That makes more sense." He turned around to face the raucous crowd. "And Mitzi gets the glory."

Dani broke out into a big smile, the gloating kind. "But she isn't going to the dance with Josh… I am."

From across the room, Katie stared at Matt and Dani. "Wonder what she wants?"

Dorie recognized the envy that lay beneath Katie's question. "Matt walked over to her."

"I'd like to know her secret. It seems like all the boys fall for her."

"You have to admit, she *is* nice," Dorie said softly, hoping not to upset Katie.

Tears formed in Katie's eyes. "I think Josh is in love with her."

"That's good, isn't it?"

Katie sighed. "I wish he felt that way about—"

"Are you—"

Katie jumped to attention. "I'm okay. I realize I'm only a freshman."

"I don't know what to say." Dorie shook her head. "I've never had feelings for a boy."

"I never did either…till Josh."

"What about Matt?"

Katie wriggled her nose. "Huh, what about Matt?"

"You don't have feelings for him?"

Katie shivered as if she had tasted a sour candy. "No way… I mean, Matt's a nice guy, but he's like a brother to me. Why, did you think I had a thing for him?"

"I wasn't sure. It's just that you two seem so close."

"We're just friends." Katie waved a warning finger. "Don't you say a word to anyone about my feelings for Josh!"

"My lips are sealed."

## CHAPTER 26

# SURPRISE VISIT

Elsa Worthington puttered around the small kitchenette of her RV. She and her husband had bought the vehicle new when he retired from the mill. They'd spent over ten years traveling around the country until his death five years ago. Since then, Elvira had begged her to scrap the RV on many occasions, too numerous to count.

Finishing up the last dish, Elsa mumbled to herself, "I'll never sell my baby. She holds too many wonderful memories."

There was a sharp knock on the door. Elsa jumped. Expecting it to be her daughter, she yelled, "Door's open."

A man stepped inside.

Elsa grabbed her chest and squealed. "Oh my! Frank Monroe, you're a sight for sore eyes!" Beaming, she rushed over and gave Frank a hug, practically squeezing the life out of him.

Frank's eyes watered. "It's just like old times," he said, returning her hug. "The boys said you were in town, so we thought we'd stop by for a visit."

"We?"

Kay Monroe reluctantly stepped into the RV.

Elsa's eyed widened and she actually gulped. "I must say, this day is full of surprises."

"How've you been, Elsa?" Kay asked uneasily.

"Good...good." Elsa motioned them to sit at the small kitchen table. "I just made a fresh pot of coffee."

Frank sniffed the air. "Is that your famous coffee cake I smell?"

Elsa just loved this man. As a boy, Frank had virtually lived at her house. Her son Will, Frank, and Rico's dad, Steven Steel, had been inseparable.

She plopped a large piece of cake in front of Frank. "Eat up," she said as she poured him a cup of coffee.

Kay declined a piece of the pastry. "I'm sorry, but I have no appetite."

"You always did watch your figure. Me, I don't care," Elsa said with a giggle. "I just fill up my muumuu." Swinging her rather large hips, she pirouetted around the kitchenette.

Everyone laughed, most of all Elsa. After catching her breath, she said, "I can see my son in you, Frankie… I mean Frank." Suddenly tears filled her eyes. She looked away.

"I miss him too. Will died way too young," he said, patting her arm. "War is an ugly thing."

Elsa wiped the tears away with her apron. "I was cutting onions earlier," she said, trying to hide her sadness. She quickly grabbed her coffee cup and took a sip. "So what *really* brings you by?"

Frank looked sheepishly at the old woman. "Never could get one past you."

Elsa sighed. "I must confess Kay's presence did make me wonder. No offense, Kay, but I know I'm not one of your favorite people."

Kay quickly said, "That's not tr—"

"Don't worry about it," Elsa said, interrupting what she figured would be an insincere declaration.

Frank swallowed a forkful of coffee cake. "I need your help with something."

Elsa rose and grabbed the coffeepot. It was an old-fashioned percolator; no fancy one-cup machine for her. She refilled Frank's cup. "So what can I do for the two of you?"

Frank took a deep breath—his body quivered. Elsa made it easy for him by asking, "Is this about Paragon?"

Kay lurched. "So the boys were right!"

Frank looked up with a shocked expression painted on his face.

"I wondered how long it'd take you to get your behind over here," Elsa said, reaching for a napkin.

Frank leaned forward. "Then you know I need your help to contact Pappy Jack."

"I see the boys told you about my conversations with Jack."

Frank scrunched his forehead.

Elsa laughed. "It's not like I can pick up a phone. I use my gift."

"Right," Frank said. "Then do you think you can get a message to him?"

Elsa leaned back in her chair. "I can do better than that. You can talk to him directly."

"That's possible?" Frank asked, not believing his ears.

Elsa stood and walked to the door. She turned the lock. Looking back at Frank, she said, "I wouldn't want my daughter to walk in on us."

Kay sighed deeply and lowered her eyes, noticeably uncomfortable.

"Elvira wouldn't understand," Elsa said, looking caringly at Kay. She opened a drawer near the sink. "Frank, can you pull the blinds? We need a darkened space."

As Frank lowered the shades in the kitchenette, Elsa brought out a small candelabra containing three white candles and placed it in the center of the table. Then she sat across from Frank.

Kay quickly stood. "If you don't mind, I think I'll visit Elvira." She opened the door. "I'll lock it behind me." The door slammed loudly.

"Sorry about—"

"She's always doubted," Elsa said, shaking her head. "It's best she left. Her negative energy would have affected your ability to reach Jack."

Frank's forehead beaded with sweat.

Elsa detected the panic in his eyes. "Not to worry. You'll be able to speak to him. Actually, you'll be able to touch him."

"Amazing."

Elsa lit the three candles. "Now give me your hands." Frank placed his hands across the table, one on each side of the candelabrum. Elsa grabbed them in hers. "Close your eyes and think of Jack."

"That's all I have to do?"

Elsa squeezed Frank's hands. "Yep, I'll do the rest. Think of your grandfather."

Frank heard Elsa's voice muttering words in a foreign tongue, words that faded quickly as she spoke, sounding distant, as though outside the recreational vehicle. His body prickled with a mild electric current that radiated from his heart, cascading through his entire being.

"Open your eyes," Elsa said softly.

Frank slowly opened his eyes. Pappy Jack and King Darius stood before him.

## CHAPTER 27

# FRIGHTENING REVELATION

Matt rushed inside the kitchen after school. His newspapers, neatly folded and packed into the orange paper sack, sat near the door. *Mom, you're the best!* When he picked up the papers, a small note card fell onto the floor.

It read: *Matty, take the large casserole out of the fridge. Put it in the oven at 350 degrees. I'll see you when I get home.*

*Love you, Mom!*

*Easy enough.* He followed the instructions and quickly rushed to his bike. It took forty-five minutes to deliver his papers. He made certain to add an extra paper for the Parkers. Why, he wasn't sure. Did they live in the mansion, or was it a hallucination?

Matt spied his father's car in front of Mrs. Worthington's old RV. *Hmm, I wonder.* He laughed when his thoughts turned to Mrs. Crow. It had been over two weeks since her mother had parked the old Winnebago in the driveway. *She has to be seething by now.*

As had become his ritual, Matt turned into the lane leading to the sad, lonely mansion. On one hand, he hoped he would never see the two children again, but on the other he had so many questions to ask them.

The place looked deserted. Matt decided to place a paper on the porch anyway, as he had the past few nights. The papers disappeared each day. He wasn't sure who took them, but he assumed it was someone in the family. He peeked through a window and saw nothing but darkness. Matt shrugged. *This is a waste of time.*

He jumped on his bike and pedaled down the driveway. As he passed the last maple tree, Nathaniel jumped out in front of him.

Matt hit the brakes hard and almost flipped his bike. After steadying the bicycle, he yelled, "You could have given me a warning!"

"Sorry. I didn't mean to frighten you."

"You didn't frighten me. It's just not very smart to jump out in front of a moving bike."

Nathaniel's face grew pale. His eyes appeared sunken in their sockets.

*Oh crap*, Matt thought, *he's turning back into a zombie.*

"Don't come back here," Nathaniel warned in a monotone.

Matt shivered, as if a cold winter wind had blown right through him.

Nathaniel headed toward the thick woods to the right of the driveway.

"Wait a minute! You can't tell me something like that and just leave," Matt yelled out. "What do you mean?"

Nathaniel turned back and faced Matt. "Never go into the mansion again...or you will die. He wants to kill you and your brother."

"Who wants to kill us?"

Nathaniel didn't answer. He quickly disappeared into the woods.

Matt jumped off his bike and followed, but to no avail. Nathaniel had vanished.

When he got home, Matt found his brother at the kitchen table, reading the paper. "How was practice?" Matt asked as he dropped the paper sack in the corner.

"You know...okay," Josh said with a grunt. "Where are Mom and Dad?"

Matt chuckled. "Dad's at Grandma's."

Josh looked up. With excitement in his voice, he asked, "Do you think he's asking her about contacting Pappy Jack?"

"Yep," Matt said, grabbing some orange juice from the fridge. He sat at the table and stared at his brother. "Josh, you look like crap."

His brother stared back. "You don't look too hot either. So there."

"I'm serious. Is the dragon wound infected again?"

"Not exactly," Josh said. "It never healed in the first place. But I feel fine."

Matt laughed. "Yeah, just like me," he said in a sarcastic tone.

Now Josh appeared concerned. "What do you mean?"

"You can't tell Mom," Matt said. Josh gave the Scout's honor sign. "I'm running a low-grade fever, and I've been hallucinating again."

Josh reached over and felt his brother's head. "Did you—"

"Yes, I took my meds."

"I'm telling Mom as soon as she walks through the door."

Matt stood up and angrily shoved his chair into the table. "Okay, then I'm telling her about the gash in your side."

Matt knew exactly what to say to get his brother's attention.

Josh rubbed his eyes and moaned weakly. "Look, *I'm* fine, but you could die if the leukemia comes back. Any kind of infection could kill you."

"I'm not an idiot. If it gets worse, I'll tell her. That's why I'm telling you now, just in case I need your help at school."

Josh ran his right hand through his thick mop of brown hair. "I don't know, Sport. You're putting me in a tough spot."

Matt placed his glass in the sink. "You tell her about me...and I tell her about you," he said with his back to his brother. "It's your choice."

"What's his choice?" Kay asked. Matt jumped; he hadn't heard his mother enter the kitchen. She looked curiously at the boys. "Is something wrong?"

Matt glanced toward Josh and shrugged.

Josh rolled his eyes. "No, we were just talking about the Halloween dance. Sport was ticked you guys didn't tell him about it."

Matt smiled. *Nice move, Josh.*

Frank walked into the kitchen. "Sorry we're late. Dinner smells great. Italian?"

"Meat ravioli." Kay opened the oven for a quick peek. "I see you got my message," she said to Matt.

In no time, they sat at the dinner table. Josh grabbed a piece of homemade garlic bread. "So where were you guys?"

Frank leaned back in his chair. "Paragon," he said nonchalantly, as if he were reporting the weather.

Matt gulped. "You're kidding, right?"

Kay took a quick bite of food and quickly reached for the pepper shaker. "Not enough pepper in the meat."

"Mom, quit trying to evade the question. You went to Paragon, didn't you?" Matt asked.

She brought her right hand up to her face. "Not me. Your father."

Frank sipped his red wine. He set the goblet down and stared intently at Matt. "King Darius said they've been watching everything that's been going on. You *did* see those children. But *why* is the big question."

Matt sighed. "Thank God. I thought I was losing my mind."

"I don't want either of you boys going into that mansion ever again," Frank stated in a firm voice, one not to be questioned.

Josh frowned. "But what about the school dance?"

"You're just going to have to miss it," Kay said abruptly.

"I was really looking forward to it." Josh's frown deepened. "I hope Dani will understand."

Frank looked over sympathetically. "I'm sure she would much prefer a quiet dinner alone with you. Make reservations at Chef Dato's."

Matt swallowed a bite of ravioli. "Nathaniel told me to stay away from the mansion," he said coolly.

"You saw that boy again?" Frank's voice held a tinge of anger.

"I go there every day. He hasn't been outside the last couple of days. But today I was minding my own business when he jumped out at me."

Kay dropped her fork. "Who jumped you?"

"It was Nathaniel, Mom. But he didn't jump me... He jumped out *at* me. And he told me someone wanted to kill me and Josh." Matt immediately regretted his revelation.

"Sport, ghosts can't kill you," Josh said, snickering. "They can only scare the crap out of you." He quickly looked at their mother, who was not amused. "Sorry about the language, Mom."

She grunted slightly and took a quick sip of her wine.

Frank jumped into the fray. "A ghost can't kill you...but Damien can."

There it was, out on the table!

Frank divulged what he had learned on the trip. "King Darius thinks Damien may still be alive and is out to get our family for destroying his plan."

Josh laughed. "Sport killed him. I saw it."

Kay took another quick sip of wine. "More than likely it's some of his followers."

"I didn't realize he still had any followers," Matt said. "I thought the elves hated him."

Frank leaned back and placed his hands behind his neck. "The king underestimated the faction Damien assembled. Anyway, he felt any followers would awaken from their deep sleep once Damien was killed." He reached for more bread.

"But if Damien is alive, wouldn't they still be under his spell?" Josh asked.

"Exactly," Frank said uneasily. "It's probably just some of his followers... Either way, I don't want you boys anywhere near that house."

Matt narrowed his eyes and groaned. "I killed him... I just wish he would stay dead. He haunts my dreams almost every night. Now he's messing with my life."

CHAPTER 28

# A FIRING

As soon as the Monroe brothers stepped into the high school, Chad ran up to them, breathing heavily. With his voice full of excitement, he announced, "Dr. Grant was fired!"

"What!" Josh couldn't believe his ears. "He's one of our best teachers."

"I agree, but he got caught by old Jasper, stealing books from the archives."

"That doesn't sound like Dr. Grant," Josh said.

Matt had his suspicions about the counselor after seeing him chase Nathaniel into the library, but he pretended to act surprised by the news. "Wow, you just never know what people are capable of."

The bell rang for homeroom. In his hurry, Matt had left his textbook for Mr. Werner's class in his locker. Although he wouldn't admit it to Katie, he actually enjoyed *Romeo and Juliet*. He got a hall pass from his homeroom teacher and rushed to his locker.

As he moved the circular knob of the combination lock, a hand touched his back. He jumped and put his hands defensively near his face, expecting it to be Rico Steel. But it was Dr. Grant.

"Don't believe them. I was set up," the psychologist said with a hint of panic in his voice. "I got a phone call. It was a woman's voice. She sounded frantic."

"Who was it?" Matt asked.

"She never gave her name. I just assumed it was Bea...Miss Butterfield. She begged me to come to the library. There had been a break-in. I was told to use the back door. The door had been pried open, and the lights were on in the basement, so I rushed downstairs. Books were scattered all over the floor. I started to clean up the mess when Mr. Green snuck up on me. He just assumed I was the one who broke in."

"I don't understand. Why would you go alone? Why didn't you call 9-1-1?"

"The woman sounded terrified. My apartment's only two blocks away, so without thinking, I rushed straight to the library."

"What did Miss Butterfield say when you got there?"

"That's just it... No one was there. When I cornered Bea this morning, she denied calling me. In fact, she seemed a little put out by my assumption that it was her in the first place."

Uncomfortable with this information, Matt asked, "Why are you telling *me* all of this?"

Dr. Grant leaned in closer to Matt. "Someone wanted me out of this school. They must have known I was getting close to the truth." He looked up and down the hall, and then lowered his voice to a whisper. "Stay away from the Payne mansion. I think there's some connection between the Parker kids, that house, and your family."

Matt leaned back against his locker. "What do you mean?" he asked, eager for an explanation.

A female voice sounded down the hall. "Dr. Grant, have you no pride? Leave this building at once!" It was the headmistress, Mrs. Watson.

"Promise me you won't go back to the old mansion," Dr. Grant said hurriedly. "It's not a safe place for you."

Mrs. Watson met up with the ousted counselor and pulled him by the arm toward the side entrance of the school. He gave no resistance. She turned toward Matt. "Shouldn't you be in class, young man?"

As Matt walked slowly back to his homeroom, he heard Mrs. Watson say disgustedly, "Dr. Grant, the only reason you haven't been arrested is the bad publicity it would give this institution."

Mr. Werner smiled that morning—something rare, to be sure. "Today we're going to do a little play acting," he announced. "I'll need a student to help me perform."

Matt wondered who the unlucky soul would be.

"Mr. Monroe," the teacher called out.

Matt looked down in an attempt to blend into his desk.

Mr. Werner coaxed him. "Don't be shy. I'm sure there's an actor in there somewhere."

Although not an introvert, Matt didn't exactly seek the spotlight. He trudged up the aisle toward the smug teacher to the sound of catcalls from his classmates.

"We'll read this section in Act II," Mr. Werner instructed. He handed Matt a small pamphlet with his lines marked in yellow highlighter.

Matt looked at his lines and took a deep breath.

"When you're ready," the teacher said.

Matt closed his eyes and breathed deeply. *If you could face a dragon, this should be a breeze.* It worked.

Mr. Werner and Matt bantered back and forth. When the English teacher read his lines, Matt looked out at the class. He expected to see his classmates making faces, but they actually appeared engaged with the reading. This gave Matt the courage to continue.

After Matt had said his last line, the class broke out into spontaneous applause. He was speechless. He looked toward Katie. She clapped her hands wildly.

"Mr. Monroe, you've been holding out on me. I had no idea you were such a talented actor." Mr. Werner patted Matt on the back. "Well done, well done indeed."

At this point the bell signaled the end of class. Matt ran back to his desk and grabbed his backpack. Katie waved to him with a thumbs-up.

Mr. Werner stopped Matt as he was on his way out of the room. "Have you ever thought of acting on the stage?"

"What?" Matt asked, truly surprised by the question.

The teacher pulled a piece of paper from a desk drawer and handed it to Matt. It was a flyer. "Tryouts for the all-class play are next month. I think you're a natural, and I want you to consider joining our group."

It was a no-brainer. Of course he'd try out. It would earn him suck-up points with Mr. Werner. Since he was a freshman, there was no way he'd be picked for a part in the play, so what harm could there be? "Yeah, I'll give it a try."

Matt ran into the library. Everyone was there...even Chad. This day was one for the ages.

Chad looked so engaged in his reading. "I should've known," Matt said, looking over Chad's shoulder.

"What?" Chad asked innocently.

Tucked inside the book was the latest copy of *Sports Illustrated.* Matt patted Chad on the back. "Read on," he said quite loudly.

A familiar loud *Shh* sounded. Miss Butterfield stood at the counter, with one finger placed to her lips.

Matt mouthed, "Sorry."

Josh looked up. He gave Matt a half smile.

Dani waved to Matt from the other side of the library. Matt approached the ex-cheerleader. She grabbed him by the arm and dragged him behind one of the stacks of books.

"What's wrong with Josh?"

Matt could not tell her the truth, so he acted clueless. "What are you talking about?"

"Look, everyone seems to be walking around in denial. He's not himself."

"What did Josh tell you?"

She didn't answer.

"Did you ask him?" Matt said.

"I did," she said loudly, her voice cracking. "He said he was fine."

"Then he's fine. I don't know any more than you do." Matt hated lying to her, but he couldn't betray his brother's trust.

Dani threw her hands up. "I don't understand you people."

They joined their friends at the table. Josh gave Matt a look of concern. Matt winked at his brother.

Without warning, Matt's vision blurred, and the room swayed back and forth. He started to hyperventilate and broke out in a drenching sweat. The energy, bit by bit, dissipated from his body. As though in slow motion, he crumpled to the floor. He lay there unable to move. He soon recognized his brother's face looking down at him.

Josh yelled out, "Miss Butterfield, call an ambulance!" His brother's voice sounded muffled to Matt, as though he were underwater.

## CHAPTER 29

# WOES FOR THE MONROE BROTHERS

Josh sat alone on an uncomfortable metal chair in the stark hallway of the Latrobe Hospital intensive care unit. A range of emotions plagued his psyche: sadness…remorse…most of all guilt. *Why didn't I tell Mom that Sport had a fever?*

Frank Monroe exited Matt's room and approached Josh. The sound of his steps echoed off the terrazzo floor. The man's eyes were red and swollen. Obviously, he had been crying.

"We just talked with Dr. Habib. Matty's really sick," his dad said in a whisper. "His white count is out of sight, and he has a fever that's not responding to antibiotics." His lower lip quivered. In a strangled voice, he said, "We called Father Vincent."

Josh's face paled and his entire body shook. "He's that sick?"

His father grabbed Josh by the arm and led him toward Matt's room.

Josh trudged into ICU #3. He could barely lift his legs. To him, they felt like heavy bags of cement. The sound of the monitors echoed rhythmically in the bare, sterile room.

Kay Monroe sat near the head of the bed. She held Matt's hand, mumbling something under her muffled sobs.

As soon as Josh entered the room, his mom stood and ran toward him. She clung to Josh. He didn't expect the strength of her hug. Kay said, barely audible, "I'm afraid we're going to lose your brother."

His mother had always been the one with deep faith and hope. She held the family together, though this night had devastated her, and Josh felt guilty. *Why didn't I tell them?*

If it hadn't been for the monitors showing Matt's respiration level and heart rate, Josh would have sworn his brother was already dead. Matt looked lifeless. He had no color.

Josh leaned over his brother. "Hey, Sport. It's me. Hang in there, buddy. You've got to fight this. Mom and Dad…and me…we aren't ready to let you go. I love you, Sport," he whispered, choking back tears. He bent down and kissed his brother on the forehead, which was hot with fever.

Suddenly the siren on the monitors sounded. Matt's heart rate had flatlined; he wasn't breathing.

"Code blue, code blue, ICU #3! Code blue, code blue, ICU #3!" blared over the PA system. In just a few seconds, a crash cart wheeled into the room, pushed by a male nurse. "Everyone out," the man yelled.

The nurse ripped Matt's shirt open. He grabbed the amulet, breaking the chain, and threw it onto the floor. It broke into many pieces. A yellow liquid from inside the amulet splattered on the floor.

Dr. Habib rushed in and charged up the paddles to shock Matt's heart, while the nurse slid a wooden board under Matt's back. The doctor yelled, "Clear."

Josh heard the shock to Matt's chest, a hollow sound, painful for him to witness. He had to get away. He sprinted down the hallway. His legs weakened, so he leaned against the wall for support. He buried his head in his hands and sobbed from the depths of his being.

Matt heard his brother say, "I love you," but he couldn't respond.

Next thing, Matt stood at the foot of the bed. He looked around and saw his parents positioned just outside the doorway. But where was Josh?

Matt ran out of the room, searching for his brother. He felt great, the best he had in a long time. He spotted Josh sitting on the floor in the hallway, propped up against the wall. Matt punched Josh in the arm. "Hey, I'm fine," he said. "Quit worrying." His fist passed through his brother's body. Matt shook with fear.

Surprisingly, he felt a hand on his shoulder. It was Nathaniel!

"I'm so sorry, Matt," Nathaniel said. "I tried to help you, but I was too late."

A bright beam of light shone behind Matt. He turned and faced the illumination, surprised that the brilliance did not hurt his eyes. He looked back to Josh and Nathaniel. Why didn't they react to the brightness? Matt, stood there stubbornly, determined not to walk into the radiance. He tried to will it away.

The light would not be denied. It traveled toward Matt and enveloped him. As quickly as it had arrived, the intense glow vanished, with Matt no longer standing in the hospital; instead, he found himself in a beautiful garden. He looked around, totally bewildered for a few seconds, until recognition flooded over him. *I know this place. It's the rose garden at the royal palace in Paragon!*

"Matt," a strong male voice called out. King Darius rushed toward him.

The elf king's long blond hair blew to the left as a slight wind puffed through the garden. King Darius bowed slightly to Matt, who returned the courtesy.

"I must ask you a question," the king said, anxiously. "Are you sure you touched Damien with the Human Element?"

Ready to answer *yes*, Matt suddenly had doubts. "I can't say for sure... I know I held the stone out, but everything went blank. I woke up on Sacred Mountain... But I can't be sure I touched him."

The king's chin sunk to his chest as he dropped down onto a marble bench. "I was afraid of that." He motioned Matt to join him.

King Darius spoke of the strange events that had occurred recently in Kingston. He told Matt all that he had learned. "Go back and share this information with your family...and keep an eye on your brother. He is quite ill."

Matt heard indistinct background noise, followed by muffled voices. Finally, he recognized Dr. Habib. "He's back. His heart rate is stable."

The doctor leaned over Matt. "You gave us quite a scare, young man. Welcome back."

The male nurse wiped up the spill caused by the broken amulet. After cleaning up the mess, he walked toward Matt's bed and adjusted the IV. "You'll be fine now," he said in a whisper. "I've removed the cause of your illness." The nurse winked as he lifted his surgical cap, revealing one pointed ear.

"You're an e—"

"You need to rest now."

A commotion arose just outside the room.

Good intentions aside, Josh believed he had killed his brother. He leaned against the wall, burdened with guilt. Slowly, he slid down the wall and slipped from consciousness.

Josh awoke with an IV in his arm. His parents sat at his side. "You gave us a scare," his father said as he rubbed Josh's arm.

Josh looked to his right directly into his mom's weary eyes. She looked awful. He tried to smile for her sake. "What happened?"

She grabbed his left hand and squeezed it.

"You blacked out," his dad said from the foot of the bed. "I think everything finally got to you."

"How's Sport? Is he—"

"He's okay...at least for now," his mom said, trying to reassure him.

Josh attempted to sit up, but after lifting his head up a few inches, he fell back onto his pillow. "He's alive?"

His mother nodded. "Yes, it's a miracle."

Dr. Habib appeared in the doorway. "Frank, can I speak with you?"

Kay jumped up. "Is something wrong with Matty?"

Quickly, the doctor said, "No, no… He's stable."

"Mom, calm down, or you're going to be in the bed next to me."

Kay's face looked pale and withdrawn. She wore no makeup and appeared to have aged twenty years overnight.

The two men quickly exited the hospital room. Alarmed, Frank asked nervously, "Amil, what's going on?"

The doctor led Frank to a small conference room.

"Matt is doing quite well. The fever has broken. The blood work isn't back yet, but I suspect we've dodged another bullet."

Frank put his head down and rubbed his weary eyes. "God, that's great news. You had me scared to death. I thought you were going to tell—"

"It's Josh. He's a very sick boy."

## CHAPTER 30

# THROUGH THE LOOKING GLASS

Dorie ambled into the library. She searched for Katie, who had volunteered to help Miss Butterfield in the library. *I can't wrap my mind around that*, she thought. Matt's collapse in the library had unnerved the entire student body, but it hit Katie O'Hara extremely hard.

Dorie spied Katie in the far corner of the library. "I thought I'd find you here. Did you hear anything new about Matt?"

Katie stepped off the short ladder. "No. I've seen Matt get sick before, but this time something's different. I'm really scared."

Dorie sat on a bench near the stack of books. "Zach told me about his battle with leukemia."

Katie picked a few books off the mobile cart and turned to place them in their correct spots on the bookshelf. "You don't know the half of it."

Dorie sighed. "I'm praying for him." Realizing that her popularity paled in importance to saving Matt's life, Dorie took a chance. "I'm going to tell you something...You can believe it or not...or you can dump me as your friend. But I have to tell you."

"Tell me already," Katie shouted.

To Dorie's surprise, Katie didn't laugh as she listened to the story about her ability to read the crystal ball. Actually, she appeared genuinely interested.

Katie leaned forward in the chair. "Since you were honest with me," she said, looking around to see if anyone else was listening, "I'm going to tell you something that tops your secret, but you have to promise to take it to the grave with you. You can't tell a soul, not even your grandma."

"Cross my heart."

Katie bent closer to Dorie. "Matt's a hero," she said in a whisper. "I know this is going to sound weird, but several of us traveled to another dimension called Paragon, and Matt saved the world from an evil elf."

Dorie frowned. "If you wanted to make fun of me, you didn't—"

Katie grabbed Dorie's arm. "I know it sounds crazy. But between the leukemia and his ordeal in Paragon, I think it may finally be too much for him."

Without thinking, Dorie blurted out, "And I thought I was weird." She saw the all too familiar look of anger on Katie's face and panicked. "I mean you're not weird... I mean—"

"I get it," Katie said, placing a comforting hand on Dorie's shoulder. "We're all a bit weird in this town."

Dorie exhaled profoundly. "I think I finally found a place where I fit in."

Katie peered at the clock. "Look at the time! I have to get going. My mother's probably waiting in the parking lot."

Katie pushed the book cart behind the counter. "Miss Butterfield," she called out, "I'm leaving." There was no answer. *I bet she's downstairs. I'd better see if she needs anything before I go home.* Katie trotted down the marble steps. She didn't see anyone.

Katie turned the corner near the wall and stopped abruptly. There stood Miss Butterfield, bathed in light. She observed the librarian slowly step into the mirror—that's right, directly into the mirror—and disappear. There was no mistaking that.

"It's official. I'm losing my mind," Katie muttered to herself as she fell sideways against a bookshelf. She didn't know what to do. She couldn't tell Matt since he wasn't available. Who could she tell? Dorie...she had to tell Dorie!

## CHAPTER 31

# DECISION TIME

Nana sat at the table, stirring a cup of chamomile tea. "Dorie, sit down. Your tea is getting cold. Your friend will get here when she gets here. That's the trouble with your generation—you're always in a hurry."

Dorie slid onto the kitchen chair. She stirred her tea aimlessly, occasionally clanking the sides of the china cup. A loud rap pounded on the kitchen door. Dorie jumped, and almost tipped the fragile cup.

Her grandmother gave her an odd look. "What are you up to?"

"Nana, please be on your best behavior. This girl is very important to me. I want to make a good impression." She walked over and opened the door.

As Katie entered the kitchen, Nana said quite loudly in broken English, "Telling truth what make good impression."

Katie smiled at the old woman, although it was half-hearted.

Blood rushed to Dorie's face, causing a slight blush. "Nana knows quite a lot about many things." Turning toward her grandmother, she said in Romanian, "But she doesn't know everything."

Her grandmother huffed. "I know friend in trouble," she said confidently in English.

"I'm sure I don't know what you're talking about," Dorie said, as she led Katie out of the kitchen.

"Sit."

It was the way her grandmother had said the word—the force, the determination in her voice—that stopped both girls in their tracks.

Nana pointed to the chairs around the kitchen table. "Who Matt Monroe?" she asked.

Dorie gulped loudly.

Nana took another sip of tea and spit it into the cup. "Tea cold."

Katie grabbed Nana's hand. "Is there something you know about Matt? Something you'd like to tell us?"

"Dat why you here…right?"

Katie gazed at Dorie's grandmother, who chuckled. Nana stood and dumped her tea into the sink. "His ball cap in basement."

Dorie didn't want Katie to get the wrong idea. "Matt wasn't here," she said quickly, almost too quickly. "I needed his cap for—"

Her grandmother clasped her hands together. "Good girl. Using gift!"

Even though Dorie had explained to Katie that she could read the crystal ball, Katie had no idea what it entailed. Dorie smiled nervously. "Yes, Nana. I'm using my gift."

Her grandmother left the room, singing.

Relieved that her grandma had gone, Dorie asked, "On the phone you said something happened at school after I left. Did Mitzi pick on you again?"

Katie rubbed her eyes and took a deep breath. "I wish it were that simple. I went downstairs to tell Miss Butterfield I was leaving. When I turned the corner, I saw a bright light coming from behind one of the stacks." Katie stopped.

"And? Come on, Katie, you can't leave me hanging like that."

"You're going to think I'm loony, but I saw Miss Butterfield…step through the mirror and disappear." She crossed her heart. "Scout's honor. Don't laugh."

Dorie didn't laugh. She didn't show any reaction at all.

Katie said in an annoyed tone, "Aren't you going to say something?"

Suddenly, Nana stepped into the kitchen. "Come."

They descended the stairs and entered Nana's world. Katie sat between Dorie and her grandmother, on a folding chair around the small table in Nana's special place. In the center of the table sat a large object covered by a fancy lace cloth.

Trying to break the tension, Dorie said, "You've heard of a man cave. Well, this is Nana's cave."

Katie grinned awkwardly.

Nana chanted in a foreign language.

Dorie whispered to Katie, "It's Romanian."

Her grandmother then uncovered the object on the table. It was a crystal ball. Dorie figured Katie had never seen one before. "This is what I told you about earlier. Nana can read the future in the crystal ball."

"Granddaughter has gift too. Her gift stronger," the old woman said, switching back to her broken English. "She only one her age can do dis."

Dorie put her head down. Telling Katie she could read the crystal was one thing, but having Katie present for a reading was quite another matter.

Her grandmother motioned toward Matt's ball cap. When Dorie attempted to give it to her, Nana put her hand up.

"No! You read! I help. He your friend."

Dorie picked up Matt's ball cap. *It's do-or-die time.* She looked sheepishly at Katie. "Well, here goes nothing," she said, barely audible. Dorie took a deep breath and placed her hands on either side of the crystal ball, allowing Matt's cap to come in contact with the mysterious orb. "Specters of the unknown, we need your help," she chanted in Romanian. "The boy who wears this hat is in trouble. Show us what we can do to ease his pain."

Katie stared at Dorie. She did not doubt her friend's sincerity, but seeing Miss Butterfield go through a mirror and now witnessing a crystal ball reading was a bit much for one day. She turned her head to break the tension, only to gaze into Nana's dark eyes; in the dim light, they looked lifeless. The temptation to crack a joke had long since passed. She didn't dare say a word.

Dorie lifted her hands. She stared at the ball, totally transfixed. In a matter of seconds, the crystal glowed a deep yellow. Katie observed a look of terror come over her friend's face.

Katie turned toward the grandmother. Nana showed no emotion. She resembled a mannequin in a department store.

"Good," Dorie said, in barely audible English.

Katie didn't know how to react. Was Dorie talking to someone?

All of a sudden, Dorie's eyes widened and her mouth dropped open. She leaned back and took a deep breath. Looking at no one in particular, she said, "Matt's going to be okay for now. But Josh… I think it's Josh who's in trouble."

"What makes you say that?" Katie asked with a shudder.

"I saw him in the crystal. He looked terrible. He was standing in an old house. Matt was with him."

Katie, shaken by her friend's answer, asked, "What old house?"

"It could be any house. I couldn't tell. But they were wearing costumes."

Both girls looked at each other. It was as though they could read each other's mind. In unison they said, "The Halloween dance."

Katie sat up straight. "They must be in the Payne mansion."

Nana spoke forcefully. "Whatever to happen will be at dance. It no accident you see dis."

Katie jumped up, bumping the table. "Then it's simple. We'll just keep them away from the dance."

Nana grabbed Katie's hand and squeezed it. "Not how work, my dear. Boys must face what to happen. Crystal can warn only. Not change."

"Then what good is it?" Katie said with a sharp tongue.

Nana did not get angry; she smiled warmly.

Dorie turned toward Katie. "Karma and destiny are in the hands of God. The crystal gives us a glimpse of the future. It's not always clear. It's up to the brothers alone to change their fate."

Nana beamed, evidently pleased with her granddaughter's response.

Katie settled back into her chair. She didn't know what to think anymore.

Dorie grabbed Katie's hand. "The dance will play an important role in their future."

The old woman said sharply in English, "Boys must attend."

As they walked up the basement steps, a strange thought crossed Katie's mind. She turned to Dorie. "Do you think the skeleton keys are for the Payne mansion?"

CHAPTER 32

# FACING THE TRUTH

The occasional echo of shoes, tapping across the hard terrazzo floor, broke the profound silence on the third floor of the hospital. Frank Monroe and Dr. Amil Habib huddled in the small conference room. The subdued overhead lighting cast dismal gray shadows on the walls.

Frank asked, "How sick is Josh?"

"His blood work is something I've never seen before. We sent a sample to the University of Pittsburgh. UPMC has some of the best specialists in the country."

Frank scrunched his forehead. "What's wrong with his blood?"

Dr. Habib hesitated. "His red blood cells are deformed. Frank, I've treated patients with sickle cell anemia, but I've never seen anything like this before."

Matt lay in the hospital bed, fiddling nervously with the ring on his finger. Unexpectantly, the top half of the ring slid to the right, exposing an odd-looking stone. Matt's eyes widened. He remembered that the ring contained a precious relic. "The broken piece of the Human Element!" he exclaimed.

His mother, who had been sleeping soundly in the chair next to his bed, jumped awake. Clearly, Matt's voice had startled her. She rubbed her eyes and yawned. "I see you're awake." She moved a few strands of Matt's hair out of his eyes.

Matt tried to sit up. "I've got to see Josh." He wanted to tell his brother about the ring.

His mother pushed him down onto the pillow. "Not now, but your dad's talking with Dr. Habib."

"Sorry to put you guys through all this," Matt said, lying back on the pillow.

His mom stood over Matt and kissed his cheek. "What are you talking about? It's not your fault the leukemia is back."

Matt didn't dare tell her that he'd had a slight fever for nearly a week.

When his dad walked into the room, Matt asked "How's Josh?"

"They're still not sure, but he's resting comfortably," his father said, as he walked over to the bed. "How are *you* feeling?"

"Good. I feel good…but I could go for some food. I'm starving."

His mother pulled the blanket up closer to Matt's neck. "That may be a while. The nurses said you're not ready for solid food, but I'll see what I can do."

Out of habit, Matt reached for the amulet around his neck. It was gone! He sat up and searched the bed.

Tuned in to his reaction, his mom said quickly, "The nurse ripped the amulet off when he pulled your dressing gown open to shock your heart."

His dad added regretfully, "It fell to the floor and smashed… I'm sorry."

Matt breathed deeply. "Good, I'm glad he broke it."

His mother wriggled her nose. "What are you saying?" she asked. "You loved that thing. You never took it off."

Matt understood her confusion, but before he could answer, the head nurse walked into the ICU room, clipboard in hand. She looked puzzled.

Kay jumped up. "Ethel, what's wrong?" She and Ethel Hightower had gone to high school together, and the two had remained good friends.

Nurse Hightower looked directly at Kay. "Oh, it's good news. Actually it's great news. I don't understand, but Matt's blood chemistry numbers are really good. I'd say they're normal."

Frank gave Ethel an odd look. "Matty almost died a few hours ago," he said forcefully. "How can his numbers be normal?"

The three adults jumped to attention when Matt said with conviction, "King Darius told me I was going to be all right. He said the amulet was poisoned."

His mom laughed nervously. "Oh, that boy loves to tease." She grabbed Ethel by the arm and walked her out of the room. "Thanks for the good news," she said, practically pushing her friend down the hall.

The nurse had a confounded look on her face as the door swung closed.

His mom ran back into the room. "When did he tell you that?" she asked in a panic.

"Tonight." Matt grinned.

His dad patted Matt on the arm. "Matty, it was a hallucination. Your fever was so high that—"

"I think I had an out-of-body experience." Matt sat up in bed. He felt invigorated.

His mom sat down on the small chair at the head of the bed. "A what?"

"I saw you and Dad. I tried to get your attention, but your eyes were glued to the doctor, so I walked out into the hall. Josh was there. I poked him, but it was like I didn't have a body. My hand went right through him."

His mom shivered.

"Yeah, it freaked me out too," Matt said, with a chuckle. "Then I saw the bright light. I thought I was dead, so I tried to run away from it. I didn't want to die." Tears ran down his mother's face. "I'm okay, Mom," he said, grabbing her hand.

"When did you talk with King Darius?" his dad asked nervously.

"The light got brighter and it came *to* me. I couldn't move. It was like the time I fought Damien. Before I knew it, I was standing in the rose garden at the Royal Palace."

"Where?"

"Odont City, Dad! King Darius called me there. He told me the amulet was making me sick. It was laced with some kind of poison. The nurse who broke the amulet is an elf from Paragon. He broke it deliberately."

A voice came from the doorway. "He talked to me too." Josh tottered into the room, tugging his IV pole behind him.

Kay jumped up. "What are you doing out of bed?"

The door opened wider, and a very anxious Dr. Habib entered. "How did you get here?" he asked Josh.

Josh looked surprised by the question. "I walked."

"That's just not possible!" the doctor said emphatically. "There's no way you could get out of that bed by yourself. You're too weak."

Josh gave the doctor a big bear hug to make a point. The doctor groaned in pain. "Okay, okay, I believe you."

"When can we go home?" Josh asked.

Definitely confounded, Dr. Habib stared at Josh, who looked healthy; his color was good and his strength had clearly returned. "I need to take a new blood sample." He grabbed Josh and marched him out of the room.

After the technician drew Josh's blood, Dr. Habib allowed him to return to Matt's room.

Kay sat in a small chair, totally drained. With both of her boys needling each other and full of energy, she looked frustrated and tired.

"Now that we're alone," Frank said, "tell me about King Darius."

"He asked me if I was sure I killed Damien," Matt said. "I told him I don't remember whether I touched the elf with the stone."

"That's what we talked about the other day, when I went to Paragon," Frank said.

Josh stood and stretched. "Whether Matt killed him or not," he said, "we have to go to the old mansion on All Hallows' Eve to face Damien…or his followers."

"No way!" Kay shouted. "Nathaniel said you could be killed if you ever returned to that house."

"We don't have a choice," Josh said.

"King Darius told me we have to go," Matt said. "We have to face our destiny at the Halloween dance, or many innocent people will die."

Frank looked lovingly at Kay. "I'm afraid they're right."

"We *can't* let them go." Tears ran down her face. "I can't go through this again."

"It's not up to us," Frank said, rubbing her shoulders. He kissed her cheek. "You and I are chaperoning the dance. At least we'll be close by."

"But they'll need help…lots of help," she said emphatically, clearly not convinced.

"We'll ask our friends. They've been through this before with us," Matt said.

"I'll talk to their parents and fill them in on what's happening," Frank said. "I'm sure they won't be thrilled with the idea."

"You'll need an army," Kay said firmly.

Just then, Dr. Habib walked back into Matt's room. "I think I'm losing my mind." Holding up a piece of paper, the doctor said in a somewhat relieved but frustrated way, "Josh's blood work is normal. His red blood cells are perfect."

Frank Monroe smiled at his friend. "That's great news, isn't it?"

"I don't understand," Dr. Habib said. "If I hadn't seen Josh, myself, I would think the blood work got mixed up. A few hours ago your son was a very sick boy. Now he's healthy as an ox?"

"Can we take the boys home?" Kay asked.

Her remark jarred the doctor out of his befuddled state. "Sure, Kay. Let me sign the release papers." He looked over to Frank. "You'll have to sign the papers too."

Kay opened up the clothes closet. "You go with Amil, dear. I'll help Matty and Josh get ready."

As the two men walked down the hall, Dr. Habib said, "I don't know what's going on. But keep a close watch on your boys. If anything out of the ordinary pops up, call me. I don't care what time of day it is."

Frank appreciated his friend's concern. "Thanks for all your help. I'll let you know if anything changes."

Amil placed his hand on Frank's shoulder. "A few hours ago I thought you were going to lose both your sons. Now it's as if they were never sick in the first place."

Josh watched their mother stroll down the hall toward the ladies' restroom. He stepped back inside Matt's room and closed the door. "We have to talk," Josh said heatedly.

"So King Darius talked to you too," Matt said, recognizing his brother's concern.

"I want to tell you that I will *never* hide your illness from Mom and Dad...ever again," Josh said with a hint of anger and desperation in his voice. "I don't care what you tell them about me. I will *never* go through the guilt I've felt since you collapsed."

"Sorry, I had no idea I was that sick. But it wasn't the leukemia after all... It was the amulet."

Josh raised his eyebrows. "The amulet?"

Matt sat on the chair beside the hospital bed. "It was poisoned."

Josh leaned back against the wall. "Who do you think poisoned it?" he asked.

A frightening thought popped into Matt's head. "It had to be someone close to the Elfin High Council."

CHAPTER 33

# MASTER PLAN

Katie stood at her locker. She reread the text message on her phone. *Tree house Friday night 6pm—meeting—real important. Matt.*

"I see you got one too."

It was Zach.

"Yeah, what do you think's up?"

"Not sure," Zach said. "I'm just glad the two of them are okay."

"That's what I heard, but I'll sleep better when I see it for myself."

Zach walked down the hall with Katie. "It's kind of creepy. Mom and Dad have been closemouthed about everything," he said. "They wouldn't let me talk to Matt. When I called his cell, it went straight to voicemail. And I've sent him over a dozen texts, but he didn't answer any of them."

Katie screeched. "Same here!"

Chad and Brian were the first ones to arrive at the Monroe farm, or at least they thought so. Bill stood in the breezeway.

"I guess I beat you," Bill said who competed in everything, down to the mundane—one of the qualities Chad admired most about Bill.

Chad tapped lightly on the kitchen door. Kay Monroe smiled broadly and waved to him through the screen door. "The boys are in the tree house."

A huge sycamore tree dominated the backyard with the rustic tree house snugly nestled in its large branches.

Following Chad up the rope ladder, Bill said, "I wonder how they're feeling."

Chad called down, "They're good. I talked with Josh the other day." He recognized the surprise on Bill's face. "Don't go freaking out. I called him."

Bill sighed. "He didn't answer when I called."

Still standing on the ground, Brian yelled up, "You worry too much. He probably didn't have his phone. You know how his mother can be. The only one worse is—"

There was silence.

"My mom?" Bill looked down. "You can say it. I know she can be a pain at times."

Chad attempted to change the subject. He could tolerate Mrs. Monroe, but Mrs. Crow was a subject he'd rather just ignore. "Think the Steelers have a chance this year?"

Bill got the hint. "What did Josh say?" he asked.

Chad didn't answer. He stepped off the ladder and climbed into the tree house. Zach, Josh, and Matt sat on the wood benches, engaged in a lively conversation.

As he stepped into the tree house, Chad bellowed, "I'm here… Let the party begin!"

Moaning could be heard on the rope ladder. Bill clearly disagreed.

Brian followed Bill into the tree house, while Chad plunged his right hand into a tub of ice filled with cans of soda pop. He pulled out a Coke and flipped the tab. Looking over toward Matt, Chad shook his head. "Are you still drinking that crap?" he asked.

Matt held an open can of Mountain Dew.

Out of the blue, laughter came from below—girl laughter. Brian looked down. A big grin spread across his face. "You guys have to see this."

Dorie hung onto the rope ladder, wrapped in its rungs. Underneath her, Katie pushed hard to help lift her friend up the ladder. Both laughed hysterically. "Do you have any athletic ability at all?" Katie hollered with a giggle.

Dorie took another step. "I'm not used to this." She looked down at Katie. "I'm not a tomboy like you."

"Move your butt," Katie yelled. She pushed up on Dorie's ample behind.

Brian looked down. "Need some help, girls?"

Dorie sighed. "My hero."

Katie grunted. "Up yours, Brian."

He climbed down and practically lifted Dorie into the tree house.

Katie followed the two. The hilarious look on her face made Matt smile. She blew damp strands of hair out of her eyes with a quick puff. "You try pushing someone that big up the ladder, and let's see how you look."

Matt quickly glanced over at Dorie, relieved to see her laughing. "Good to see some things never change," he said.

Katie's mood flipped one hundred and eighty degrees. "Seriously, how are you guys doing?" she asked.

Matt hugged her. "It was touch-and-go for a while, but we're both good."

Zach handed each girl a cold soda, then sat next to Dorie, who scooted close to him.

"Where's Sean?" Katie asked.

"He couldn't make it. Had to work in his grandfather's garage tonight," Josh said. "I told him I'd fill him in later."

Dorie scanned the small room. "This place is neat. I've never been in a tree house before."

"Or climbed a rope ladder either," Chad said, waggling his eyebrows.

Dorie shrugged off his remark with a disarming smile.

Brian looked around the room. "Looks like everyone's here. Let's get this show on the road."

"Not *everyone's* here," Josh said.

They looked oddly at him, especially Bill. "Who's missing?" he asked.

"I invited Dani."

Chad slapped him on the shoulder. "It's about time. That girl's crazy about you."

Matt gritted his teeth and turned toward Katie, who stared tearfully at Josh. Matt sympathized with her. She had a big crush on his brother. Katie had never said anything, but he knew. For a boy so intelligent, his brother was totally clueless when it came to girls.

"Josh, are you up there?" a soft voice called from below.

Josh rushed over to the rope ladder and waved. "Climb up."

Dani had no trouble climbing the ladder. In a short time, the ex-cheerleader stood in the entryway.

Katie scowled at Dani.

If looks could kill, Matt figured he was about to witness a murder. To make matters worse, Josh fetched Dani a soda and sat next to her.

"Now we can start," Josh said.

Matt took his brother's cue. "We have some very creepy information to share with you." Everyone sat silently, giving him their complete attention. Matt bit his upper lip and then blurted out, "Damien may still be alive."

"That's just perfect," Chad said, nervously slapping his right leg.

Brian stared at Matt in disbelief. "But we saw you kill him."

"It may just be some of his followers that we'll have to deal with," Josh said as he leaned back on the bench.

"I can't believe anyone would be stupid enough to still believe in him," Chad said, scratching his head. "I thought those elves were pretty smart."

Dorie inhaled sharply.

Surprised by her reaction, Matt asked, "Didn't Katie fill you in on our recent trip?"

"Yes, but—"

Katie pounded her fist on the wooden bench. "Did you think I could make something like that up?"

Dorie flinched. "No...but it's just so unbelievable," she said meekly.

Chad walked over to the tub of sodas. He pulled out another can of Coke and snapped the tab open. "Who else did you tell about Paragon?"

Matt detected a tinge of anger in Chad's voice.

"No one," Josh said defensively.

Chad wiped sweat from his forehead. "Thank God for that. It sounded like the whole effin' school found out about it. And that wouldn't be cool."

Bill sat quietly, listening to his friends trade jabs back and forth. Then he raised his hand.

*Here we go*, Matt thought.

Chad chuckled. "This isn't school. You don't have to raise your hand. If you have something to say, just say it."

Bill cleared his throat. "I'm still getting used to the idea that there are elves and parallel worlds. But what exactly do you want us to do?"

Matt raised his eyebrows. *That's it? Nothing else to add?* Maybe Bill had changed. Probably not, but he could hope.

"The Halloween dance is where King Darius thinks the confrontation will occur," Josh said in a strong voice.

Dorie nervously tapped her fingers on the bench. Katie urged her, "Tell them. Tell them what you saw."

Dorie sat in silence. When she looked up, she appeared ready to cry and swallowed hard. "Everything *will* happen at the Halloween dance," she said, barely audible.

"How do you know that?" Bill asked.

"I saw it."

Matt watched the panic in her eyes, like a cornered animal that didn't know where to run. "Don't be afraid to tell them," he said compassionately.

"I can read the crystal ball," Dorie said between gritted teeth. She lowered her head.

"You can do what?" Chad asked.

Dorie looked up sheepishly. "I can read the crystal ball."

Chad groaned. "What are you, some kind of gypsy girl?" When no one laughed, Chad leaned back in silence.

"I had Matt give me a personal item of clothing," Dorie said. "So I could do a reading."

Chad snickered. "What did he give you, an old jock?"

"Quit while you're ahead, bro," Brian said sharply. "This isn't a tryout for Comedy Central."

"If you're going to goof around, you can leave," Josh said, clearly miffed. "I can't believe you're being such a jerk. You were in Paragon. You know how dangerous Damien's followers can be."

Bill jumped to Chad's defense. "Don't you guys get it? When Chad's nervous, he gets a little goofy."

Chad punched Bill's arm. "Wait a minute—"

Brian grabbed his brother. "Can you let the girl talk? I'd like to hear what she has to say." He motioned Dorie to continue.

She rubbed her eyes. "Matt gave me his ball cap. I need a piece of clothing that's come into contact with the subject."

"Oh, so now he's a subject," Chad said.

Josh threw a handful of popcorn at Chad. It worked. The boy finally quieted down.

Dorie appeared more relaxed; the tenseness in her jaw had disappeared, and she no longer hyperventilated. "I saw Matt and Josh in an old house. They were walking down a wide hallway. It seemed to go on forever. There were many rooms on either side."

Zach spoke up. "Do you think it was the Payne mansion?"

Chad rolled his eyes. "That old house isn't that big."

"I don't know where it was," Dorie said. "But at one point they walked through a mirror. Then I saw them standing in a garden." She shivered. "A black figure and a dragon appeared out of nowhere."

Matt moaned. "Not the dragon!"

Dorie leaned back. "That's where the vision ended."

"That's it?" Dani asked, disappointment evident in her voice.

Katie's facial expression changed; her forehead furrowed, and her cheeks reddened. "You didn't tell me you saw them walk through a mirror," she said angrily.

Dorie looked puzzled. "I thought I did. But why does that matter?"

"Don't you remember what I told you?"

Josh leaned forward. "What are you talking about?"

Katie wriggled her nose. "You know everyone blamed Dr. Grant for stealing books from the library," she said. "But I believe someone else did it. I think it was Miss Butter—"

Dani interrupted. "What does that have to do with the Halloween dance?"

"If you let me finish," Katie said, visibly irritated, "I'll tell you." She looked around the room. "The day after Matt got sick, I volunteered to help at the library...to keep my mind busy and all right, I'll say it...to earn brownie points with Miss Butterfield."

Bill whistled. "That's one tough cookie. I hope it was worth the effort."

"No, it wasn't... No surprise there, but here's where it gets weird. The other day, when I was ready to leave the library, I couldn't find Miss Butterfield. So I went down into the basement, and what do you think I saw? You could guess for ten years, and you'd never get it."

Dani cleared her throat. "Did you see Miss Butterfield step through the mirror and disappear?"

Matt observed an instant look of regret on Dani's face, as her cheeks turned pale.

Total silence fell over the group. Katie grunted in disbelief. "Yes, but how—"

Dani squinted. "I guess I'd better come clean."

Chad cried out, "Yeah, that would be nice."

Katie clenched her jaw and stared angrily at the ex-cheerleader.

Dani took a deep breath, then blurted out, "Miss Butterfield is from Paragon."

Katie slapped the wooden wall. "And you didn't think that was important enough to share with us?"

"I had no idea you even *knew* about Paragon till Josh told me yesterday," Dani said. "Let alone that you'd been there."

"When I told you about our trip to Paragon, you acted like you'd never heard of the place," Josh said angrily.

Dani's eyes shined glossy with tears, while Katie sat with a smug expression on her face.

Bill jumped up. "Leave her alone. She had no choice."

"What do you know about this?" Josh asked.

Bill's face blanched. "It's not—"

"I'll tell them," Dani broke in. "Bill was sworn to secrecy."

Matt watched Chad's reaction; he was ready to explode. Chad yelled at Bill. "You were ticked off because you weren't told about Paragon. What a hypocrite! You were lying to us all this time."

Bill looked down and said nothing.

Dani spoke directly to Josh. "I've been watching Miss Butterfield, and..." She hesitated and took a deep breath.

"Go on, we're listening," Josh said in a gruff manner. He pulled away from Dani and leaned back against the wall.

"I don't want to hear anymore." Chad threw his hands in the air. He stood up and headed for the doorway of the tree house. "You're all a bunch of liars."

"Quiet!" Matt yelled as loud as he could. "Everyone calm down." There was total silence. "I'm sure Dani has a good explanation. Give her a chance to talk."

Chad folded his arms and leaned against the doorjamb.

Dani took a few deep breaths to help regain her composure. "Miss Butterfield is the faculty advisor for the cheerleaders. One day after practice, Mitzi sent me to the library to get some papers from her. I couldn't find Miss Butterfield anywhere. I figured she must be in the basement, so I ran downstairs. That's when I saw her walk through the mirror. I freaked."

She had everyone's attention, most especially Katie's.

"I flew upstairs, and guess who was sitting at the front desk."

Katie answered. "Miss Butterfield?"

Dani nodded.

"How is that even possible?" Chad asked, shaking his head in disbelief.

"Then I'm not going crazy!" Katie blurted out. "The same thing happened to me."

"Miss Butterfield pulled me aside and told me she was from another world called Paragon. She was sent here by Miss Witherspoon." Looking at Josh, Dani added, "She told me that I could tell no one, not even you."

"Then why does Bill know?" Chad asked, visibly irritated.

Now it was Bill's turn in the hot seat. His face turned pale, and he fidgeted on the bench. "I can see people's memories," he divulged, while looking down at the floor. "There, I said it."

"This is so amazing," Dorie murmured.

Chad gave Bill the strangest look. "You can do *what*?"

"If I hold someone's hands, their memories are transmitted to me," Bill said. "Dani grabbed my hand the other day after her fight with Mitzi. She unknowingly transferred her memories to me."

Brian lowered his head and groaned. "This is getting really weird."

Dani squeezed Josh's right hand. "I'm sorry I kept this from you. Miss Butterfield told me that you and Matt were very ill, and she was here to help you… She said I had to keep her identity a secret."

Josh stared at Dani with sad eyes. He didn't say a word.

Finally, Matt broke the silence. "I guess I understand," he said, although he wasn't totally convinced by Dani's story. Attempting to get the meeting back on track, he asked Dorie, "So why do you think everything happens at the Halloween dance?"

"Because you were wearing Halloween costumes."

"Okay, what were we wearing?" Matt asked.

Dorie gave him a quizzical look.

"It's not that I don't believe you," Matt said, even though he had his doubts. "It's for everyone's benefit. What were our costumes?"

"I understand… I'm not offended," Dorie said. "You were Robin Hood, I think. And Josh was dressed as Zorro."

Josh gasped. "It's legit."

Chad jumped in. "You think you could read my future?"

Josh sneered. "If you don't quit fooling around, I know your future—getting tossed out of this tree house on your head."

Dani took a quick sip of soda. "I may as well put all my cards on the table. I have another secret to share with you tonight."

Josh slapped his forehead. He leaned back against the wall and mumbled to himself.

Dani placed her hands over her eyes and took a deep breath.

"It must be something terrible," Katie blurted out.

The tension in the small room had intensified. Matt and the others sweated profusely in the cramped space.

Dani looked directly into Josh's eyes. "I'm a necromancer."

"Is that even legal?" Chad asked, chortling wildly.

Bill glared at his friend. "Do you even know what a necromancer is?" Chad looked down. "I didn't think so," Bill said disgustedly.

Matt scratched his head. "What is it?"

Dani peered at Matt. "It's someone who can communicate with the dead." She glanced at Josh, and pleaded, "I didn't ask for this."

Josh, evidently floored by this additional revelation, leaned back against the tree house. He stared straight ahead in silence.

Katie just had to dig. "I thought you were going to tell us you were a witch," she said with a snort.

She had crossed the line. Josh glowered. His look of disappointment put Katie in her place.

"I guess I'm a necromancer too," Matt said in defense of Dani.

Dorie laughed quite vigorously. "And I was worried you would think I was strange because I can read a crystal ball."

"Mom and Dad told me that about a hundred years ago two kids were killed in Kingston," Matt said.

"Are you talking about Nathaniel and Annabelle Parker?" Dani asked.

Josh lowered his head and then looked up with the most intriguing grin. Pointing toward Matt, he said, "They're Sport's new best friends."

"Hey, I didn't know they were dead."

Chad freaked. "What the heck?"

"I've been talking with them over the past month," Matt said. "I had no idea they were dead."

Chad grunted. "Well, aren't we a bunch of misfits," he said with a deep sigh. Maybe it was the way he had said it or the look on his face, but everyone snickered, and then broke out into roaring laughter.

Dani grabbed Josh's hand. Katie looked away. "I've seen Miss Butterfield pop through the mirror many times," Dani said. "I always assumed she went to Paragon. But I don't trust her."

Katie chimed in. "Neither do I."

"Do you think maybe she's meeting with Damien's followers?" Matt asked.

"I can't be sure," Dani said. "But there's just something about her."

Matt stood up and stretched. "Let's not take any chances. Don't tell her what we know...just in case."

"Yeah, let's keep a close watch on her at the Halloween dance," Katie said.

"I have a better idea. Let me invite her to join our group," Dani said. "That way, we can surprise her if she tries to pull something."

Chad agreed. "I think that's a great idea. If she *is* working for Damien, we can blindside her."

Matt tossed his empty can of Mountain Dew into the metal garbage can. "Let's meet again. Josh and I will talk to our mom and dad and see if they've heard anything new." He looked around the room. "Thanks for your help."

Katie walked across the small room and stood only inches from Dani. Matt held his breath. *What is she up to?* Katie gave Dani a big hug. This shocked everyone in the room—especially Dani, whose eyes opened wide.

"You defended me when no one else would," Katie said. "And I never thanked you. I'm sorry."

Dani hugged her back. "It's okay. I'm just glad we're on the same team."

As they climbed down the rope ladder, Katie looked up at Dani. "It's kind of a shame you're not a witch though."

Matt wondered where this was going.

"And why's that?" Dani asked nervously.

"If you were a witch, you could turn Mitzi into a big, warty toad!"

CHAPTER 34

# The Summit

Elsa did her best to make the small RV presentable for the meeting. She expected a large group; even her daughter had agreed to attend. There was a loud knock on the door. Elsa looked at her watch.

"And it begins," she said as she opened the metal door.

Elvira stood there expressionless, holding a tray of cookies. Not surprised by her daughter's formality, Elsa said, "You didn't have to knock. My home is your home."

"I don't think it's proper to just barge in."

Elsa sighed. "Set them on the counter, dear." She loved her daughter. But if Elvira hadn't been born at home, Elsa would have sworn she'd gotten someone else's child.

In a matter of minutes, the tiny RV teemed with people; even Kay Monroe was there. She brought a tray of scallops wrapped in bacon.

Elsa rubbed her hands together. "That looks wonderful. You can set it on the table."

Verletta Roundtree, Zach's mom, brought her famous crab dip. The luscious aroma filled the trailer.

Jean and Joe McGuire were the last to arrive.

"Help yourself to drinks and goodies," Elsa said, relishing her role as hostess. "Don't be shy."

The parents appeared relaxed, almost festive, considering the severity of the situation. Conversations buzzed around the RV.

Finally, Frank called for order. "Okay, folks, please gather 'round. Bring your drinks."

They sat on the benches that marked the living-room portion of the RV. When Frank took his seat, the conversations stopped. "First of all, I'd like to thank Elsa for hosting this meeting," he said. Everyone clapped politely. Elsa blushed slightly, enjoying her five minutes of glory.

Frank's demeanor turned serious. "Let me get right to the point. We thought all the danger was over after Paragon. But as I explained on the phone, trouble is brewing." He took a quick sip of water. "Elvira is the only one who hasn't experienced the magic of Paragon. So for the rest of you, this meeting with King Darius won't seem that impossible."

Elsa chimed in, "I explained everything to my daughter. She understands—"

"I'll try to keep an open mind," Elvira said, rather unconvincingly.

"That's all we're asking," John Roundtree said with an encouraging nod.

Frank looked at Elsa. He took a deep breath. "Take us to Paragon."

"Everyone, hold hands," Elsa said, reaching for Frank and Elvira.

Elsa relished the fact it was her duty and honor to open the gateway to the mysterious world. She cleared her throat. "You'll be startled at the phenomenon you're about to experience. Your body will remain here, but your mind will travel to Paragon. Now close your eyes," she said with a slight giggle. She looked around the room. "No peeking."

Elvira moaned slightly.

Elsa droned hypnotically. The words were alien to all present. At one point during the chant, Elvira said, "My body's tingling." Elsa felt it too, although nothing more than exaggerated prickles.

"Open your eyes," she said in a whisper.

Amazement, it was sheer amazement, especially for Elsa's daughter. The group stood in the rose garden just outside the royal palace in Odont City.

Elvira's eyes stuck out like two small moons, her mouth agape. "Where are we?"

A strong masculine voice answered her promptly. "You are in Odont City, the capital of Paragon."

King Darius stood only a few feet away. "Welcome back. It is so good to see you."

"Thank you, Your Majesty," Frank said, bowing slightly to the king.

"No formalities needed today, my friend."

CHAPTER 35

# DIVERSION

The massive tent looked like a huge mushroom that had sprung up overnight on the front lawn of the Payne estate. The early afternoon sun reflected brightly off the white canvas, and the distinct sound of heavy pounding reverberated across the field as large sledgehammers drove steel pegs into the hard ground. At times, sparks ignited from the metal-to-metal contact. It took professional roustabouts, with the help of a select group of students from the academy, only a few hours to erect the impressive structure.

"That thing's awesome," Matt said, staring at the nearly completed work.

"It can hold over three hundred people," Sean said rather proudly, wiping sweat from his forehead.

By this time, most of the workers had gathered around the galvanized steel tubs filled with cold drinks. Sean grabbed a can of Coke. "Not bad for a day's work." He tapped Josh on the shoulder. "You look wiped out."

Josh breathed heavily, while he poured a bottle of cold water over his head. "I'm just out of shape."

Sean yawned and stretched his arms. "Can you believe it's eighty degrees on October thirty-first?"

"I can't remember a hotter Halloween. But it'll be great for the dance tonight," Matt said, knowing full well they would miss the festivities.

Chad stepped out of the tent, toting a large sledgehammer. Bill followed him.

"That was fun," Chad said excitedly, as he joined the group. "I think I'm going to run away and join the circus. It would be a blast to be a roustabout for a year or two."

Bill groaned. "You'd fit right in, that's for sure. In fact, I bet you'd be the ringleader in no time."

"Forget roustabout," Josh said with a mischievous smile. "I think Chad would make a great circus clown."

Chad reached into the tub and pulled out a can of soda. He took a handful of ice and snuck up behind Josh. He pulled the elastic waistband on Josh's shorts and shoved ice down his underwear. Josh jumped around like a rabbit till the ice fell through his pants to the ground.

"I may not get mad"—Chad grinned and shook a finger at Josh—"but I always get even." He took a sip of his soda and spit it out. "God, that's awful."

Chad held a can of Mountain Dew.

The boys sat under the partial shade of one of the large crimson maples. The tree had lost over half its leaves, allowing rays of sunlight to filter through the many holes now present in the leafy canopy.

"So is everybody set for tonight?" Sean asked.

"We'll meet here at five," Josh said. "And once the party's going full throttle, we'll go inside the mansion."

Chad looked around. "I heard they're placing the displays in the lower level of the house."

"Yeah, that's right," Frank Monroe said, who seemed to have popped up out of nowhere. "We've roped off the upstairs. Once we're all together, we'll go inside and explore."

Sean scrunched his forehead. "What makes you think the action will be upstairs?"

Josh patted him on the back. "Remember, Dorie saw Matt and me standing in what looked like an upstairs hall."

Three catering vans from Dino's Sports Bar pulled up in front of the house. Chad watched as the caterers carried large tubs of food into the tent. "I know Mitzi's a jerk, but you guys have to admit, she does know how to throw a party," he said. "I'm starved."

"There'll be plenty of chicken wings for everyone," Dr. Monroe said. "By the way, Chad, how's Brian doing?"

"He's ticked off, that's for sure," Chad said, tossing his empty pop can into the trash bin. "I can't believe he has the flu. We sure could've used his help tonight."

"It's an odd time of year for the flu," Dr. Monroe said. "But it's best he stays in bed. We'll have enough help."

When they got home, Josh leaned against the kitchen sink and downed a quick glass of water. His face looked pale.

Concerned about his brother, Matt asked, "Are you sure you're okay?"

"I wonder if I'm coming down with the flu," Josh said with a sigh. "I feel drained." He trudged up the back stairs. "I'm going to take a quick nap."

Matt followed him into the bedroom and started to strip. "I'll take my shower now. You can take yours later."

Josh nodded and flopped onto his bed. He conked out quicker than a flickering candle hit by high winds.

Matt stepped into the shower and instantly felt a sense of foreboding. *Calm down*, he thought. *God is with you.*

He lost all sense of time as the hot water poured down his dirty, achy body. The room filled with steam. After drying himself with a towel, Matt walked over to wipe the foggy mirror above the sink. Mysteriously, a smudged message appeared on its surface: *This is my time.* It was as though someone had written the words with a finger. Matt blinked, and the message disappeared. He raced back to the bedroom.

Josh lay in a deep sleep, snoring loudly. Matt shook his brother, but he didn't budge. Finally, after repeated prodding, Josh stirred. "What's up?"

"Time to get your shower." Matt grabbed his phone from the nightstand. It read 5:10 p.m. *I couldn't have been in the shower that long, could I?* "Josh, we're late."

His brother jumped up and winced. "Let me take a quick shower."

After his shower, Josh walked into the bedroom, wrapped in a large white towel. Peering at Matt, he snickered. "Who are you supposed to be?"

"Robin Hood, remember?" The attached brown cape swayed around his green outfit as Matt shifted his hips.

Josh laughed uncontrollably.

"What's so funny?" Matt asked.

"You look more like Peter Pan."

Josh dressed quickly while Matt looked at himself in the mirror on the dresser. "You're right. I can't wear this."

"It doesn't matter. Look at me. I'm supposed to be Zorro."

"You *do* look like Zorro. Cool look. But I look like some pathetic lost boy...in tights."

Josh raised his eyebrows. "It's odd... Mom never came up to wake us."

Matt's heart fluttered. He ran out of the room and down the steps into the kitchen. He spied a handwritten note on the table.

*We thought you could use the extra rest. Get to the dance when you can. We'll be waiting for you. Love, Mom.*

Josh parked the car in the Kingston Club parking lot. The school had gotten permission to use the club's lot and the field, if necessary.

Climbing Kingston Club Road, Josh struggled to keep up. He breathed heavily, and his legs dragged with each step.

"Maybe you should've stayed home."

Josh gave Matt the 'what are you talking about' look. "Yeah, right. You may be facing Damien, and I would just sleep through it."

"Hey guys, wait up," Bill yelled. He, Chad, and Sean raced down the Crow driveway.

Matt gave them a thumbs-up. "Cool costumes."

"Thanks, man," Bill said. "It was a tough decision, but we settled on zombie apocalypse."

Totally impressed with the look, Matt said, "Really, you guys look fantastic."

Chad wrapped an arm around Matt. "And who are you supposed to be...Peter Pan?"

Matt grunted and pulled away. "Robin Hood. Can't you see I'm Robin Hood?"

Sean raised his eyebrows. "If you say so."

At this point Josh jumped into the conversation. "I see you're late too."

"Can you believe we slept in?" Chad said. "I guess that job wore us out more than I thought."

*Why did we all sleep in?* "Are Grandma and your mom at home, or did they leave for the party?" Matt asked.

Bill's jaw dropped. "No, they're gone!"

Matt groaned. "Don't you see...something's up? Your mother definitely would have wakened you."

CHAPTER 36

# The Halloween Dance

The blare of rock music drifted down the narrow lane.

The boys arrived at the Payne mansion to find hundreds of kids roaming the grounds. Chad kicked at small pieces of gravel in front of him. "It looks like we're the last ones to get here."

They stood in front of the large circus tent, waiting for their friends. The boys decided to enter the tent. Festive music filled the canvas structure. Many of their friends greeted them cheerfully; however, no one had seen Zach and the girls.

"Do you think they went into the house?" Matt asked, as they exited the tent.

"No way," Josh said. "They know the plan. No one goes inside till everyone's here."

Two kids stood on the front porch of the mansion—Nathaniel and Annabelle. Matt ran toward the house. "Hi, guys. What do you think of the party?"

"Interesting music," Nathaniel said with a slight sneer. "But not to my taste."

Annabelle scurried to Matt and gave him a big hug. "I'm so happy you could come." She looked at the four boys approaching the porch. "Are these your friends?"

Matt figured the other guys couldn't see the children. "Yes, but—"

Chad waved. "Cool outfits. Who are you supposed to be, the Parker kids?"

Nathaniel looked confused. "What a silly question. Of course we're the Parkers... This is our house."

Matt stared at Chad. "You can see them?"

"Have you been drinking something stronger than Mountain Dew? Of course I see them."

The boys introduced themselves to the Parkers.

"Good to make your acquaintance," Nathaniel said. "I'm Nathaniel Lee Parker and this is my little sister, Annabelle Louise."

Annabelle giggled. "Charmed, I'm sure."

Chad whispered to Bill, "They're good actors. I wonder where the school found them."

Bill gave Chad an odd look. "Chad, I don't think you understand. They *are* Nathaniel and Annabelle Parker."

Sean and Josh said nothing, but as usual, Chad had to run his mouth. "It can't be. They're dea—"

Bill elbowed Chad in the side. "It's good to meet you," Bill said, extending his right hand to Nathaniel, who shook it rather formally.

Josh smiled tentatively. "Excuse us for a minute."

"See you inside," Nathanial said. With a polite wave, the two children entered the house.

"I can't believe you see them," Matt said.

Chad looked around and whispered, "I thought they were dead."

"They *are* dead," Josh said emphatically. "That's what makes this so weird."

Bill leaned against the porch railing. "We meet two dead kids. And now they ask us to go inside... I don't think so. We should wait."

Chad's patience wore thin. "Wait for what...Christmas? Maybe we misunderstood, and everyone is waiting for us inside the house."

Josh's right eye twitched as he rubbed his nose. "I know we were supposed to meet them in front of the tent. We're late. Maybe they got tired of waiting and went inside. If the five of us stick together, what could happen?"

Matt bit his lip lightly. "What could happen? Gee, I don't know, maybe we could get killed!" he mumbled.

## CHAPTER 37

# SEPARATION

Matt opened the front door with ease and stepped inside the old house. "Wow, it looks amazing!" he said, totally impressed with the work done by the students and faculty.

"Cool!" Chad said. "I can't believe how authentic this place looks. It's awesome."

The house had been converted into a nineteenth-century country manor. The antique furniture highlighted the metamorphosis. From their wooden frames to their satin cushions, the pieces reflected that time period perfectly.

Matt poked his brother. "Look at the costumes the actors are wearing. They're unbelievable."

"Matt, we're up here," Nathaniel called from the stairs above the landing, which led to the second floor of the old mansion.

"Let's go upstairs," Matt suggested.

Josh grabbed his arm. "We have to wait for the others."

"It'll be okay as long as we stick together," Matt said, practically begging his brother.

"I guess we could look around for a few minutes, but then we come back downstairs till the others get here," Josh said, clearly nervous. "All right?"

Bill, the ever-vigilant one in the group, asked, "Wasn't there supposed to be a rope to prevent anyone from going upstairs?"

No rope barred their way. In fact, nothing blocked the stairway, allowing anyone access to the restricted area of the house.

"Hey, weren't our teachers supposed to be the actors in the house?" Sean asked suspiciously. "I don't recognize anyone."

"You're right," Bill said. "Something's definitely off."

Chad slapped his friend on the back. "You think so? You'll find out when you're with the Monroe brothers everything is off-kilter."

As the boys ascended the steps, a booming voice cried out, "Where do you think you're going?"

Matt turned around to face a familiar foe. The stodgy Mr. Hardcastle, dressed as a vampire, stood with hands on hips. Matt had to admit the costume was way cool.

"We thought we'd take a quick peek upstairs," Matt said, trying to appease his teacher.

He could plainly see the look of total disapproval on the man's face—even under a ton of makeup.

"That area is forbidden to *all* students. And unless I am mistaken, you are a student."

Ignoring Mr. Hardcastle, Josh led the boys upstairs. Halfway up, he turned around and said defiantly, "If you didn't want us upstairs, you should have roped it off. We'll be back in a few minutes."

Matt loved his brother's bravado. But it was no surprise to him when Mr. Hardcastle yelled from the bottom of the steps, "Take one more step, and I'll make sure the five of you get detention."

Matt turned to Chad. He recognized the ornery look in his eyes. "I got this," Chad said.

Chad looked down toward Mr. Hardcastle. "This isn't school property. It's owned by the Monroe family. And we're allowed to go anywhere we want. If you have a problem with that, talk to Dr. Monroe."

Matt gave Chad a high-five and bounded up the rest of the steps. Matt looked back to observe Mr. Hardcastle's reaction. A cold shiver ran through his entire body, for a foreboding figure of a man stood next to Mr. Hardcastle, a man whose face Matt could never forget—Colonel Parker.

Bill tapped Matt on the shoulder. "Did you see old Hardcastle's face?"

Sean sighed loudly. "Yeah, but did you see that sour old man standing next to him?"

"That's Colonel Parker." Matt noticed the confusion on Sean's face. "Yeah, he's dead too."

Sean looked back. "Oh." He said nothing more.

Nathaniel poked Matt. "Who is that man standing with Papa?"

"Never mind him," Chad said. "He's just one of our teachers. He thinks he's a bad ass, but he's just a horse's ass… If you know what I mean."

Matt found Nathaniel's reaction comical. "Your friends are very interesting," Nathaniel said with a wicked smile. "Their choice of vocabulary is quite entertaining." Nathaniel grabbed Matt by the arm. "Come, let me show you the upstairs library."

The boys entered the first room on the left. It was a huge library. Hundreds of books filled the shelves. Gas lamps illuminated the room.

Bill dashed to one of the stacks of books. "These are antiques." He gave Matt an odd look. "I thought the upstairs was unfinished."

Josh grabbed Bill's arm. "It is unfinished," he whispered. "This isn't real."

Bill picked up a book, a first edition of *A Tale of Two Cities* by Charles Dickens. "You're telling me this isn't real?"

Nathaniel walked over to Bill and grabbed the book. "Please don't touch Papa's things, or I could get into a lot of trouble."

Sean ambled across the hall. "This colonel guy must be an avid hunter. Look at all the trophies on the wall," he called. "There's a fourteen-point buck. It's awesome."

Bill and Chad darted across the hall to join Sean in the study.

Nathaniel ran after them. "Don't go in there! It's Papa's private study."

The heavy wooden door slammed, leaving Matt and Josh alone in the library.

Hearing the library door close, Bill quickly stepped toward the study's doorway; however, the door slammed in his face. He tried the doorknob—locked. "Nathaniel, do you have a key?"

No one answered. Nathaniel had vanished.

Sean said, "Great! I can't believe we were stupid enough to leave Josh and Matt alone."

Bill took out a penknife. "Never fear, a Scout is here." He knelt on the floor and tried to pick the lock.

Chad snickered. "That'll never work."

After a few tries, the lock clicked open. Bill looked up with a huge smile plastered on his face.

"You were lucky this time," Chad said with a scowl.

Sean opened the door. "Quit your bickering! We've got to find Josh and Matt." They ran across the hall. Sean turned the doorknob, and the library door opened easily; however, the room was empty. "Where'd they go?" Sean asked.

Both brothers jumped when the door slammed. Josh rushed to the solid oak door. It opened with a simple twist of the doorknob. "For a minute, I thought we were trapped."

Josh stepped out into the hall. He turned back to Matt with a confounded expression on his face. "You've got to see this."

Matt peered into the hall. "I don't believe this," he said, stunned by the sight. The hall appeared three times as wide and went on for what seemed like forever.

"There's definitely black magic written all over this," Josh said.

Matt got a sick feeling in the pit of his stomach. "Didn't Dorie say she saw us walking down a long hallway with many rooms on either side?"

Josh leaned against the wall. He didn't say a word.

Nathaniel appeared in the hallway and waved the brothers forward. "Down here," he called.

"You know we can't trust him," Josh whispered. "This is a trap. I just know it."

Matt grabbed Josh's arm. "I agree. But let's see where he takes us."

## CHAPTER 38

# DECEPTION

Katie paraded through the tent, disguised as Annie Oakley. She pushed up on the brim of her cowgirl hat and scanned the crowd. Patience not being one of her virtues, she folded her arms and tapped her right foot anxiously. *They should have been here by now*, she thought, frowning.

Dani, dressed as a princess, peered through the crowd. The expression on her face revealed that she hadn't seen the boys either.

The girls met Dorie and Zach, who stood watch outside the huge tent. "They're not inside?" Zach asked.

"No," Katie said in frustration.

Dani walked over to Dorie. "Love the costume. Are you supposed to be a gypsy fortune-teller?"

Katie grunted. "How original."

"No one's seen Josh or the other guys," Dani said. "You don't think something's happened to them?"

"They're fine," Dorie said confidently. "Remember, it was dark and there was a full moon when they confronted the dragon."

Zach pointed toward the driveway. "Hey, there's Matt's mom and dad."

The four teens ran to the SUV. Dr. Monroe had barely gotten out of the car when he was accosted by the teenagers. Dani looked inside the car. "Aren't Josh and Matt with you?"

Kay Monroe looked beyond the teens, toward the tent. "What? Aren't they here?"

"Nobody's seen them," Dorie said, with a worried look on her face.

Grandma Elsa, Miss Butterfield, and Elvira Crow joined the group.

"You're late," Grandma Elsa said. "But more importantly your *sons* are late."

"You haven't seen them either?" Kay inquired.

"Have you seen William?" Elvira asked, nervously playing with her necklace. "He's supposed to be with Josh and Matt."

"You don't suppose they went into the house without us, do you?" Katie asked.

Dani walked toward the front porch of the mansion. "Have you seen Josh and Matt?" she hollered.

Katie followed Dani's gaze to the front porch. "Who are you talking to?"

"The Parkers," Dani answered.

Katie saw no one standing on the porch. "Oh."

"Who?" Mrs. Crow asked. Obviously she didn't see the children either.

Katie grinned sheepishly. "She sees dead people."

Everyone stood silent for a few seconds. Then Grandma Elsa asked, as if it were normal to speak to dead people, "What did they say?"

"Nothing." Dani ran toward the porch. Turning back, she shouted, "They just ran inside. I think they're up to something."

Katie and company met up with the others in front of the mansion. The group quickly came to a decision to enter the old house. They stood inside the entranceway and looked around, hoping to see the boys.

"Is that Mr. Hardcastle dressed as a vampire?" Katie asked.

"Good evening," the stern teacher said. "Welcome to Kingston Manor."

Mr. Werner stood in the parlor, his costume quite ornate. Elizabethan, to be sure.

Katie sauntered into the room. Mr. Werner smiled rather pompously. "Welcome to our little soiree. Let me introduce myself. I am William Shakespeare." He pointed to a gentleman across the room. "That is my good friend, Charles Dickens."

The man portraying Mr. Dickens leaned against the fireplace mantel and bowed. He wasn't a teacher, but his intricately designed costume set him apart from the others.

"And this lovely young lady seated in front of us," Mr. Werner said, "is none other than Miss Jane Austen."

Katie recognized her as one of the senior students at the academy. Katie decided to play along. "It's an honor to meet all of you. I do hope you enjoy the party," she stammered, and then asked, "Have you seen Matt Monroe?"

Mr. Werner shook his head. "Can't say that I have. But before this day is o'er and the melancholy orb of night sinks below the horizon, you shall experience the mysterious."

Astonished by the English teacher's theatrical delivery, Katie hoped to impress him, but all she could come up with was an uninspired "I hope you have a nice night." She gritted her teeth. *How could I say something so brainless?* She wanted to crawl under the large area rug in the center of the parlor and hide.

Frank and the other adults searched every room on the lower level of the house. "Oliver, have you seen my sons?" Frank desperately asked the history teacher.

"Yes. They were looking for you. Before I could stop them, they ran upstairs."

The entire group immediately headed up the stairs.

"I told them it was off-limits, but they didn't listen to me," Mr. Hardcastle called after them. "They're undisciplined, you know."

"Thanks, Oliver," Kay said, looking down toward the befuddled teacher. "We'll deal with them."

To Frank's surprise, a young boy suddenly stuck his head out of one of the rooms.

Elsa screamed, "It's Nathaniel Parker!"

Nathaniel appeared frightened and slammed the door. Frank and Kay rushed to the door and opened it. They spotted Matt and Josh in the far corner, standing with Nathaniel.

"There you are," Frank said to his sons. "Why didn't you wait for us?"

Suddenly, Matt, Josh, and Nathaniel disappeared.

"Where'd they go?" Kay asked apprehensively.

The Roundtrees and the McGuires stepped inside the room. Tom Roundtree asked, "Did you find them?"

Kay wailed. "They were here, but they vanished right in front of our eyes."

Hearing the mournful scream, Katie attempted to enter the library, but the door slammed shut, leaving her and the remaining members standing out in the hall.

Katie jiggled the doorknob.

"Is it locked?" Dorie asked.

"Yep," Katie said.

Zach pushed her aside and pounded on the door. "Dad, are you guys okay?"

There was no answer.

Katie experienced a piercing cold sensation pass through her. Nathaniel stood in the hallway, covered in blood. As he emitted a high-pitched yelp, Katie's skin sprouted goose bumps. In a flash, he laughed wildly. "Does he think this is a game?" she asked.

"I think he does," Grandma Elsa said soberly.

Nathaniel waved them forward. Katie and the other teens ran down the hall, but the boy vanished as they approached him.

Grandma Elsa hollered, "Wait for us."

Katie heard crying from one of the rooms. With the door opened wide, she saw little Annabelle on her bed, covered from head to toe in blood. Bill sat beside her with a look of terror on his face.

Grandma Elsa ran into the room and cuddled the little girl. Mrs. Crow and Katie's mom followed. When Mrs. Crow reached her son, she stomped her foot in anger. "Why didn't you wait for us?"

Suddenly the door slammed. Annabelle and Bill vanished from sight, leaving Grandma Elsa, Mrs. Crow, and Katie's mother trapped inside.

Katie turned the doorknob, but to no avail. It would not open. She pounded on the wooden door. "Mom, are you all right?"

There was no response.

Katie fell against the door, shaking. She, Dorie, Zach, Dani, and, of all people, Miss Butterfield remained.

"I suggest we stay out of the rooms," the librarian said urgently.

Dani nodded. "Good idea."

They hurried down the hall, passing one room after another. Soon the hall ended with three doors: one on the right, one on the left, and one directly ahead.

Katie asked, "Which door do we take?"

CHAPTER 39

# Right, Left, or Center

"Which one do we take?" Katie asked again.

Dani stared at the doors. "Look, the ones on the right and left have modern locks. But the door in the center needs a skeleton key." She turned to Katie. "Give me the skeleton keys."

"What skeleton keys?" Katie answered innocently.

Miss Butterfield sighed loudly. "The keys Miss Witherspoon sent you."

Katie couldn't believe her ears. "All this time you knew it was Miss Witherspoon!" She stared angrily at the librarian. "I thought it was Mitzi. I suppose you thought it was okay to drive me nuts wondering who sent them."

Miss Butterfield sighed once more. "I just found out myself, so get over it already."

Dorie said meekly, "Excuse me."

Katie lost control. The past two months of her dealings with Miss Butterfield came to a tumultuous climax. She raised a fist and marched to the librarian. "You're not a nice person, and I don't like you."

Miss Butterfield stepped backward until she bumped into the door. "You'd better back off, young lady. Remember, I'm your teacher," she said, her voice trembling. "Don't you forget that."

Dorie tried once more. "Excuse me."

Dani grabbed Katie from behind. "She wasn't allowed to tell you. Miss Witherspoon forbade it."

Katie sighed. "I don't need those stupid old keys anyway. I have a magic wand that opens locks," she said in an uppity manner. "Miss Witherspoon gave it to me."

Dani leaned against the door on the right and banged her head lightly against the wood.

"What's your problem?" Katie said, as she removed the wand from the belt on her costume. She said the magic words and waved the wand. Nothing happened.

Dorie said for a third time, "Excuse me." This time a little louder, but she was ignored once again.

Dani looked up. "Magic won't work in this house…at least not tonight."

Katie screamed. "I didn't bring the keys."

Zach moaned. "Great, we're screwed."

"I knew you couldn't be trusted with something this important," Miss Butterfield said. "I have no idea what Leota was thinking."

Katie kicked the center door in frustration.

Miss Butterfield snorted. "Very mature, Miss O'Hara."

"Excuse me." Dorie held something in her hand. "You told me to carry the keys, don't you remember? You said your outfit didn't have any pockets."

Katie looked up and saw the keys dangling from Dorie's hand. "I-I forgot. There's been so much on my mind." She grabbed the small brass ring that held the three skeleton keys. "Thanks," she whispered to Dorie.

"Which key should I use?" Without anyone answering, Katie chose the middle key. *Middle key for middle door.*

Katie bent over and placed the key into the lock: a perfect fit. She looked up with a shocked expression on her face. "It won't turn."

Miss Butterfield's patience had reached its limit. She pushed Katie aside. "Here, let me. You probably don't have the key inserted completely." She shoved the key farther into the hole. Suddenly, the librarian jumped back and grabbed her hand. "I've been burned!"

A red welt rose on the palm of the librarian's hand.

"Here, let me try." Dani placed her hand on the key and turned it hard to the left. Suddenly she jumped back and rubbed her right hand. "It felt like I stuck my hand into an electric socket!"

"Of course, what was I thinking?" Miss Butterfield grabbed Dorie. "Since you were the one who brought the keys, you must be the one to open the door."

"Are you crazy?" Dorie asked. "I don't have a death wish."

Katie stepped up to her friend. "Try it." Hoping to lighten the mood, she said, "Your hair couldn't get any frizzier, so not to worry."

Dorie smirked. "Thanks a lot."

Zach glared at Katie. He walked over to Dorie and whispered, "You can do it."

After a fleeting moment of doubt, Dorie picked up the keys, which had fallen to the floor. She turned toward Zach, who crossed his fingers and encouraged her to proceed. Dorie gritted her teeth as she inserted the middle key. She slowly turned the key to the left. There was a loud click. Dorie pulled on the door, and it opened toward them.

CHAPTER 40

# Room of Mirrors

Matt and Josh meandered down the expansive hall. They passed room after room. At last, Matt noticed a door on the right opened wide. He looked in and spied Nathaniel, who stood in the middle of the circular room with his arms crossed and a grin on his face.

Matt whispered, "You don't suppose he thinks this is a game, do you?"

Josh mumbled, "I never thought of that. He *is* just a kid. Maybe the colonel tricked him."

Nathaniel waved Matt forward. "This is the way," he called.

As soon as they stepped into the room, the door slammed. Matt turned around. "Where's the door?"

The door had vanished, replaced by a mirror. Of course, Nathaniel had disappeared again.

Josh grabbed his brother. "This isn't funny. How do we get out of this one?"

Matt scanned the circular room. He counted; there were eighteen identical full-length mirrors. As if on cue, the mirrors began to rotate around the room, like horses on a carousel.

The spinning started out slow, but then it sped up. The light in the center of the ceiling pulsated like a disco ball. The faster the light beat, the faster the mirrors spun. The phenomenon quickly overwhelmed their senses.

Josh moaned. "I'm getting sick." He dropped to the floor.

"Close your eyes." Matt darted across the room toward Josh.

"Look out!"

Too late—Matt rammed into a table placed smack-dab in the center of the room. The wooden platform didn't budge. He took the full force with his thighs.

Matt looked down at the tabletop. Five tarot cards sat there—five Death cards! In frustration, he swept the cards off the table, exposing a keyhole in the center of the wooden surface. Matt needed a skeleton key to turn the lock. He thought of the keys Katie had received in the library.

By this time, Josh lay flat on the floor, barely conscious.

"Hang in there, Josh. I think I can stop the mirrors. There's a keyhole on top of the table."

Josh looked up. "But we don't have a key."

"Maybe not... But I have something much better."

Josh turned on his side. He watched as Matt pressed the ring from Paragon down flush with the keyhole. The spinning mirrors slowed. Within seconds, they stopped completely.

Matt sat on the floor next to his brother. "This ring has saved our butts too many times to mention," he said, flashing his hand in the air.

Josh sat up. His face had regained some color. "Totally weird. It was like I was being hypnotized by the light or something."

"Matty, where are you?" a voice called out. *Mom!* Suddenly, the boys glimpsed their parents, who stood inside one of the mirrors. Another voice called out. Katie and Zach stood in that mirror. The boys kept hearing the calls of many of their friends, teachers, and family until each mirror but one reflected someone they knew.

A dark figure emerged in the last mirror: a man wearing a black overcoat. His red mutton-chop sideburns looked like flames on the side of his face, while his thick eyebrows arched over his murderous eyes. "I warned you to stay away, you disgusting boy."

Josh stood up and staggered toward the mirror. "Who the heck are you?" he asked, his voice full of frustration.

"Colonel Parker," Matt whispered.

The colonel laughed madly. "Before this night is over, everyone you see in these mirrors will die."

Josh pulled off one of his boots. "Screw you," he screamed angrily. He tossed the boot toward the reflection of Colonel Parker. It broke the mirror into a thousand pieces.

Matt expected to hear glass shattering, but he didn't expect the sound of a shoe bouncing down a set of stairs. He walked over to the broken mirror and stuck his head through the space. "It's a stairwell!" He turned back toward Josh, who hobbled toward him. "Let's get out of here."

Matt held on to his brother as they stepped through the broken mirror. A subtle tingle rose up his spine. He heard Dorie's voice in his head: *I saw you walk through a mirror out into a garden.*

## CHAPTER 41

# The Skeleton Key

In frustration, Chad threw a book across the library, barely missing Bill. It hit one of the stacks. The binding disintegrated, and pages flew everywhere. "How could we be so stupid?"

"Did you have to do that?" Bill asked as he bent down to pick up some of the loose pages.

"What?" Sean asked, with a sour look on his face. "You're worried about a book at a time like this?"

"Well, he didn't have to destroy it," Bill said. "I'm sure it was priceless."

Sean slammed his hand down on the maple table in one corner of the room. "Who gives a crap about that book! It's probably just an illusion anyway."

Chad snickered. "Bill, you are so out of touch. Only you would worry about a book. You can be such a dork."

Bill darted toward Chad, his fists clenched. Chad grabbed him, and the two tussled.

"Cut it out, both of you," Sean boomed out. "Concentrate on why we're here. We have to find Josh and Matt."

Chad released Bill and leaned back against one of the stacks. "This is just like when we were in Paragon," he said. "It seems no matter what we do, there's no way to help Josh and Matt."

Without warning, the books and furnishings in the library faded away, and within a few seconds the room sat bare. The door popped open.

The boys raced into the hallway.

Nathaniel stood at the far end of the hall, laughing and waving his arms.

Sean gritted his teeth. "I'm going to wring his neck."

"He's dead, so I don't think it'll hurt him one bit," Bill said.

"Maybe not, but it'll make me feel good."

The boys chased Nathaniel down the hall. He made a quick right turn and dodged into a room. Not just any room—the room of mirrors. The boys met Zach and the girls, who stood in the center of the room with Miss Butterfield.

"Where did Nathaniel go?" Sean asked.

Dani sprinted to Sean and hugged him. "Oh, so happy to see you!"

The door slammed shut. The light in the center of the ceiling pulsated, and the mirrors began to spin around the room.

Dorie held on to the table in the middle of the room to keep from falling. Katie struggled to join her at the table. One by one, the others fell to the floor at the perimeter of the room, seemingly unconscious.

"I think I'm going to be sick," Katie said. She looked down at the tabletop and saw the keyhole in its center. Katie slumped to the floor, while Dorie clung to the table. "There's a keyhole on top of the table. Do you still have the keys?"

Dorie stood, wobbly, and attempted to pull the keys out of her pocket.

"Put the key into the hole," Katie urged.

"Which key?" Dorie asked, as she fumbled with the keys.

Katie felt nauseous. "Pick one, any one."

With great difficulty, Dorie attempted to insert one of the skeleton keys into the keyhole. Of course, it was the wrong one. As she pulled it out, the keys slipped from her hands and flew across the room. Katie crawled toward them.

By this time, just about everyone had passed out except for Chad. "What are you doing?" he asked weakly

"Trying to get the keys," Katie said.

"What keys?"

Katie pointed. "The ones lying over there."

Chad spied the keys, which lay against the wall of the circular room. "I'll get them," he said as he crawled toward them.

After some difficulty, he retrieved the skeleton keys and tossed them to Katie. She in turn handed them to Dorie, who by this time was quite pale. Dorie inserted a key and turned it to the right. There was a loud click, then the light stopped pulsating. As soon as the mirrors ceased moving, one of them slid open, revealing a stairway.

# CHAPTER 42

# THE GARDEN

Wisps of wind carried the smell of flowery perfume.

"We must be heading outside," Josh said as he slowly descended the spiral staircase with Matt's help. The fragrant aroma floated up the stairwell. "I can smell flowers."

"It's late October," Matt said. "All the flowers have been killed by frost."

"I know, but I smell flower blossoms," Josh said weakly.

"It must be another form of black magic."

A narrow wooden door hung ajar. The wind blew it back and forth. The sound of a squeaky hinge rang out as the brothers stepped through the opening into a lush garden.

Matt's stomach clenched. "Dorie said we'd run into a dragon in the garden."

"I'm really tired," Josh said in a subdued voice. "I have to sit."

Matt pointed. "There's a bench just ahead." It was a struggle, but he guided his brother to the center of the garden. Josh quickly slid onto the bench. He looked paler.

"Are you okay?" Matt asked.

"No... I'm not. I feel nauseous... I don't have any energy."

As soon as Matt settled in next to Josh on the bench, the temperature fell sharply. The white blossoms of the azalea bush next to the bench withered and turned brown.

A man's voice came from somewhere in the garden. Matt looked up. In the far end of the garden stood Colonel Parker.

Thinking of the children, Matt blurted out, "Why are you holding Nathaniel and Annabelle captive in this house?"

The man chuckled. "They are free to go anytime they wish." As he spoke, the aura around the colonel turned deep red. "I tricked them into leading you and your friends back into this house."

"Why?" Matt asked, tired of the games. "Why are you doing this?"

The man answered coldly, "To kill you."

"What did I ever do to you? I don't even know you."

The colonel stared defiantly but said nothing.

Josh rolled off the bench onto the ground. "I'm going to throw up," he said, breathing deeply.

Matt stooped down near his brother, frantic, unsure what to do.

After a few moments, Josh lifted his head. "I feel better now." With Matt's help, he rose. He used the wooden slats for leverage and plopped down hard onto the bench.

Matt looked around for the colonel. He had disappeared.

Seemingly out of nowhere, Katie, Zach, and the other teens, along with Miss Butterfield, appeared in the garden. They ran toward the brothers.

Sean whooped loudly. "I was worried we were too late."

Unexpectedly, a violent tremor shook the ground. Matt tumbled down on his face, Josh plopped off the bench, and the others swayed and fell as the earth rolled under their feet. The tremor created a deep fissure that ran the full width of the garden, a gulf nearly twenty feet deep and fifteen feet wide, isolating all of them from the house.

CHAPTER 43

# CONSPIRATOR REVEALED

"How could I have been so careless!" Elsa screamed, gripping one hand tightly with the other.

Elvira whimpered. She turned the doorknob and yanked, but the door wouldn't open. "It's locked…or jammed."

Jane O'Hara stood motionless. "We should have known better."

Elsa walked her daughter to the bed. She placed her right arm around her as they sat. "Calm down. We'll figure this out." Her tone was soothing.

Jane leaned against the wall. "This is a repeat of what happened in Paragon."

All at once, the room shook violently and the study door burst open.

"My God, it's an earthquake!" Elvira screamed frantically.

When the room stopped shaking, Elsa noticed Frank, standing in the hall.

Elsa jumped from the bed. "Where are the boys?"

Dejectedly, Frank said, "They vanished from the room."

Nathaniel appeared at the end of the hall. He held a clenched fist in the air. He opened his fist and a monarch butterfly emerged, flitting in the air around him. "Follow the butterfly to your sons," he said, before fading away.

The butterfly led them through the room of mirrors and down the steps into the garden. They stood only twenty feet from their children, but a chasm blocked their way.

Out of nowhere, a flash of blue light illuminated the entire garden. Madame Violet from Paragon's Elfin High Council stood regally before them.

Matt sprinted to the stately elf and wrapped his arms tightly around her. "I'm so happy you got here when you did. Colonel Parker was going to kill us."

"What are *you* doing here?" Miss Butterfield asked the elf. "Haven't you done enough damage?"

"Your plan has been thwarted," Violet said, confidently.

The librarian walked toward Violet. "What are you talking about?"

"It was you who poisoned the amulet," Violet said. Tears formed in her dark blue eyes. "I knew you admired Damien, but why do this?"

Bea Butterfield threw her hands in the air. "How dare you! Everyone knows it was you who tried to kill Matt. As far as the amulet goes, you wouldn't let that thing out of your sight till you put it around that poor boy's neck."

Both were convincing, but one of them was lying. Matt watched Bill sneak up behind Miss Butterfield.

Bill lunged forward and grabbed the librarian's right hand. He fell to the ground, struggling for air.

Matt ran over to him. "Are you okay?"

Bill gasped. He grabbed Matt's shirt and pulled him close. "She's lying," he said weakly. "Miss Butterfield's lying."

"Sister, we had you followed," Violet said. "Our spy told us you traveled through the mirror many times. But I know for a fact you did not go to Odont City."

"You think you know everything," Miss Butterfield said angrily. "I put up with your arrogance when we were children...but no more." She strutted around the garden. "Damien tried to raise elves up, but you couldn't see it. You're the traitor...a traitor to all elves."

A forlorn expression overcame Violet's countenance. "No, Bea, you are the traitor...to all creation. How could you be so foolish?"

Katie looked from one to the other. "I'm confused."

Miss Butterfield grunted. "Are you that dim-witted? I'll never know what your beloved Leota Witherspoon sees in you." She glared at Matt. "And you! I thought I'd choke on my words every time I had to speak to you."

Matt stared in disbelief. Miss Butterfield was a follower of Damien!

The colonel appeared behind Madame Violet. He grabbed the elf and tossed her across the garden. She landed hard, then lay still and lifeless.

Matt, frozen with terror, heard a loud moan from his brother. "I can't take the pain, Sport," Josh said. "My side is killing me."

Miss Butterfield turned to the teens. "First I'm going to deal with the Monroes, then I'll deal with each of you...one at a time."

"Not gonna happen, lady," Chad yelled as he ran toward her. With a barely perceptible wave of the librarian's hand, Chad rolled on the ground, writhing in agony.

Miss Butterfield's eyes burned with hatred. With her arms outstretched, she froze the teens in place.

The librarian turned back toward Matt. "Since you are going to die anyway, I may as well tell all. Yes, *I* was the one who poisoned the amulet. My sister had no idea she marked you for death when she placed it around your neck. It was working perfectly, causing the hallucinations, slowly driving you mad...slowly killing you. Somehow Darius figured it out and saved you once again. If that charm hadn't been destroyed, you would be dead."

Colonel Parker walked toward Miss Butterfield. "You did very well, my dear."

"Thank you, Master," she said, beaming with pride.

## CHAPTER 44

# RETURN OF THE DRAGON

Thunder sounded, and lightning streaked across the sky. A black mist engulfed the colonel. When the vapor faded away, the man's true identity revealed itself—Damien!

Matt stammered, "It-it can't be you… I killed you!"

"Not quite," said Miss Butterfield. "You never touched my master with that stupid stone. It was I who transported you to Sacred Mountain. I removed Damien to safety before anyone else found you there."

Matt could not speak. He had failed on all counts.

"Dear, step aside," Damien said. "I am going to kill this little pest once and for all with one jolt of my power."

"Gladly," she said, clapping her hands excitedly.

Katie screamed, "Leave him alone." She shook in terror, helpless with her feet frozen in place.

Miss Butterfield pulled Matt toward Damien. "Oh, how I've waited for this day. That nosy Dr. Grant almost spoiled my plan, but I fixed him."

"He said he was framed!" Matt said with a shudder.

A nasty smile played across the librarian's lips. "He thought he was so smart."

Matt's parents and the other adults hollered frantically from just a few feet away.

"I have relished this day," Damien said. He knocked Matt to the ground with a simple wave of his hand. "Prepare to die." He said something unintelligible and then raised his right arm toward Matt.

It was as though everyone had screamed *No!* in unison. Damien paused. He looked back at Matt's mom and dad with an evil sneer. "Watch your son die."

This short delay foiled the evil elf. Someone shot out from behind a nearby shrub with unbelievable speed and hit Damien squarely, knocking him to the ground. Incredibly, it was Rico Steel!

Bea Butterfield grabbed Rico roughly by the arm. "I'll teach you to interfere!"

Damien recovered quickly. His red eyes blazed with anger. "He's mine. Don't touch him."

"Leave him alone," Josh said weakly.

Damien turned toward Josh, who lay helpless on the ground. "Want to go for a spin, pretty boy?" He levitated Josh and tossed him high into the air, out of sight. The sound of breaking tree branches could be heard in the distance. Matt trembled for his brother.

Damien turned toward Matt. "One down, one to go," he said gleefully.

Seeing an opportunity, Rico attempted to escape. "Not so fast, you little worm," Damien said, freezing Rico in his steps. "You're going to pay dearly for your interference. I'm going to enjoy this."

He pointed a finger toward Rico, who instantly twisted in pain, screaming wretchedly. Soon Rico lay silent and still. "I'll let you rest. I don't want to kill you too quickly," Damien said with a smirk.

A loud screech sounded in the woods. It echoed across the valley. In an instant, a large creature swooped down and landed on Miss Butterfield, crushing her. There was no scream, no struggle. She died instantly.

Matt stared at the beast; it was the dragon!

The creature turned toward Damien, who quickly vanished.

The sinister beast approached Matt, who did not cower, although his right leg shook wildly.

Matt remembered the piece of the Human Element inside the ring. The dragon stood only a few feet away. "Nice boy. Don't be afraid." He slid the ring open, exposing the Human Element. If he could only touch the beast with the stone, he could kill it. The big question was whether the dragon would kill him first.

The dragon sat motionless. Then it brought its head down close to Matt and growled, exposing its many razor-sharp teeth. Matt looked into the beast's eyes. *That's odd. They're blue, not red.* He gently petted the dragon's nose, then turned his hand over and touched the creature with the stone. The dragon writhed in pain, letting go with a roar that practically deafened Matt.

A bright light engulfed Matt and the dragon, blinding everyone else in the garden. In the light, Matt observed something magical. The dragon lifted into the air. Bluish-white light revolved around the beast, which appeared to shrink and dissolve away. What remained of the dragon floated gently to the ground.

The earth shook, and the gulf closed between the two halves of the garden. Once the bright light was extinguished, there was an amazing discovery. Matt was fine, but more astounding to all, Josh lay in front of his brother, covered in Matt's cape.

Matt placed his hand on his brother's chest and felt shallow breathing.

The death of Bea Butterfield had released the teens from her spell, and they raced to the brothers. Dani knelt beside Josh, who began to stir and opened his eyes.

Dani beamed. "You're all right now!"

Josh attempted to sit up. Looking confused, he asked, "Sport, what happened?"

Chad scratched the side of his head and sighed in astonishment. "You mean you don't remember any of this?"

Frank and Kay Monroe rushed to Josh's side.

Matt dashed to Rico. The boy lay motionless, with Madame Violet at his side. The stately elf had not been killed by Damien after all.

Of all the strange things that had gone on, one puzzled Matt most: *Why did Rico save me?*

"We knew you needed help," a voice behind him said.

Nathaniel and Annabelle stood only a few feet away.

"You got Rico to help *me*?"

"You weren't our only visitor," Nathaniel said, as he patted Matt on the back. "That boy came to the house many times after his great-grandfather died."

"Our stepfather wanted you dead. That's why we didn't want you to come back to the mansion," Annabelle said.

"We didn't know about that evil woman. I'm so happy I enlisted your neighbor to help us," Nathaniel said. "I had to be careful; our stepfather watched my every move."

"Rico?" Matt asked once more. "You got Rico to help…me?"

"Yes, I talked with him on the porch on many occasions," Nathaniel said. "He told us that you saved his life. You know, Rico is jealous of you and your family. He said you had the perfect life."

Annabelle jumped into Matt's lap. "He actually admires you."

The news from the two children shocked Matt.

Rico moaned and rolled onto his side. "What happened?"

Madame Violet stepped back, leaving room for Matt to kneel beside the hero. "You were one of the good guys," Matt said.

Nathaniel knelt at Rico's other side. "You saved Matt," he said. "Your great-grandfather would be very proud of you."

"So it's all over?" Rico asked.

"Not quite," Sean said, as he helped Rico to his feet. "With the Monroe brothers, it's never over."

Madame Violet huddled everyone together. "We feared Damien might still be alive. Now that he has exposed himself, it won't take long for us to track him down."

Frank Monroe appeared a bit jittery. "How can you say that? Look what he put us through the last time."

It was Matt who spoke up. "Dad, last time Damien had the Human Element. It was his shield."

"That's right," Madame Violet said. "He has no shield today. There is nothing to protect him and no place to hide. It's only a matter of time before he's captured."

Music played in the distance. "Is the party still going on?" Chad asked.

Matt snickered. *You can always count on a party boy.*

A blue light flashed, and Madame Violet glowed. It was not the normal glittery look of elfin skin. Light literally radiated from her being. "Go to the party and celebrate. This is a happy day." She smiled lovingly at the teens and vanished.

Elvira Crow shivered. "I don't think I'll ever get used to all this weird activity."

Elsa Worthington grabbed Bill. "I for one think you all should go and have some fun. You've earned it."

Bill looked at his mother, who hugged him. "Go...go have a good time," she said.

Bill ran to catch up with Sean and Chad. "Let's party!" he yelled.

Elsa Worthington placed her hand on her daughter's shoulder. "I'm proud of you," she said in a low voice. "Give the boy some space. Let him be free to make his own choices. You have to let him go."

"I know... But he's all I have left of his father." Mother and daughter embraced.

Zach grabbed Dorie's hand. "Ready to party?"

Dorie hugged him. "This will be my first Halloween dance."

"Our car is out front," Frank said. "We'll take Josh home."

Dani held Josh's hand as he limped out of the garden with Matt's cape tied around his waist. They walked out the side gate so as not attract attention.

Katie turned to Matt. "Are you coming?"

Matt stood in a stupor. He finally realized she was talking to him. "Yeah, in a minute... Go ahead and I'll join you later."

"I don't want to leave you alone."

Matt hugged Katie. "I'm not alone."

Katie scrunched her forehead. Then she raised her eyebrows. "Oh! Are Nathaniel and Annabelle here?"

"Can't you see them?"

She shook her head. "No."

"Go, I'll catch up with you," Matt said.

Katie smiled and ran to join up with Zach and Dorie.

As his friends exited the garden, Matt spotted Nathaniel and Annabelle and strolled over to them.

"So what are you guys going to do now?"

"We'll stay here. That's all we've ever done."

Annabelle gave Matt a huge hug. "At least *you're* here now."

Matt hugged her back. "I'll be here for as long as you need me."

The ordeal had taken its toll on Matt. Worn out, he sat down on a nearby wooden bench. "But you guys do know it's not 1901, right?"

Nathaniel sat down beside him. "The last thing I remember was our stepfather grabbing me in the high pasture. Then everything went dark until I saw you walking up the driveway."

"When did you realize something was off?"

"When you delivered the paper, Papa threw it into the woods. I retrieved it and read the date."

"You don't remember anything from 1901 till the present?"

"Nothing. That's why you seemed odd to me, from the way you dressed to the silly things you said."

Annabelle giggled. "Yeah, you were funny."

Matt sighed. "So to you, it's still 1901."

Nathaniel nodded.

"This is so wild," Matt said, shaking his head. "What happened to your mother?"

"He hurt her," Annabelle said, in a sad voice.

"The colonel?" Matt asked.

"That's why we ran away," Nathaniel said. "We were afraid of him."

"He can't hurt you anymore," Matt said. "That man tonight wasn't your stepfather. Your real stepfather killed himself years ago. He couldn't cope with what he did to you."

Nathaniel stared, wide-eyed. "So he's gone forever?"

"Forever," Matt said reassuringly.

A soft voice called out, "Nathaniel, Annabelle…where are you?" It was a loving voice.

A woman dressed in nightclothes entered the garden, carrying an oil lamp. She had a peaceful smile.

"Mama, is that you?" Annabelle called back.

The woman set the oil lamp on the ground. She held her arms out to the children.

"Where have you been, my darlings? I've been looking everywhere for you."

Annabelle ran to her mother. They embraced. Nathaniel stood in place. "Go ahead," Matt said, pushing him toward his mother. "She's going to take you home."

Nathaniel slowly approached his mother. She looked up with a warm smile and loving eyes. After some hesitation, he leaped into her arms, weeping tears of happiness.

The gentle woman gazed at Matt. With her arms wrapped around her children, she said, "I don't believe we've met. I'm Loretta Parker. Thank you for helping my children."

Nathaniel and Annabelle waved at Matt. They turned and walked arm in arm with their mother to the gate that led out of the garden.

Matt smiled as he heard their mother say, "Wait till you see our new home. It's beautiful."

Nathaniel asked, "Is there a pond?"

"Yes, Son. And you have a rowboat all your own."

"Are there any dolls in my new room?" Annabelle asked.

"It's full of dolls, sweet girl. More than you can imagine."

Matt experienced a stirring of triumph deep within his soul, as he observed the happy reunion. "See you later," he called after them. Matt wasn't sure they had heard him because the three faded into the mist as he spoke.

CHAPTER 45

# JUST DESERTS

Matt walked through the old house. The earlier transformation had vanished, leaving no sign of the grand interior. The narrow halls were in terrible need of fresh paint. Two of the four bedrooms had no doors, exposing them to anyone who stumbled by. Matt looked at his phone. It was 9:00 p.m. As he progressed through the upstairs of the mansion, the buzz of people carried up the steps. From the landing, he saw that the dance was going full tilt.

"Welcome back, Mr. Monroe," a deep voice said.

Mr. Hardcastle stood at the bottom of the stairwell. His face lacked its normal sneer. Even so, Matt descended the stairs cautiously, sure Mr. Hardcastle was about to scold him severely. He was mistaken.

The stern teacher smiled as Matt approached him. The man actually patted Matt on the shoulder. "I think we got off to a bad start," Mr. Hardcastle said. "My friend Tom Roundtree told me about your recent problems, and he vouched for you. He said you were a good student and a good boy." The man extended his right hand.

Matt wasn't sure how to react. "Thank you, sir." He shook hands with his former nemesis.

Mr. Hardcastle leaned toward Matt. "By the way, your essay on John Adams is one of the best I've ever read. Great job," he whispered.

Matt beamed. Indeed this was a special night. "I really appreciate that, sir."

"There you are," a familiar voice cried out. It was Sydney Mason, dressed as a vampire. Matt held back a snicker, for she looked more comical than scary.

"Great party, isn't it?" Matt said, totally oblivious as to whether it was or not.

"Have you seen Katie?" Sydney asked with concern.

"I think she and Dorie went to the main tent for some food."

Sydney pouted. "She dumped me for that new girl."

"That's not true. Dorie doesn't have many friends, and Katie's only trying to make her feel welcome." Aware that Sydney felt deserted, Matt thought a little fib was called for, and added, "Besides, I think she was looking for you."

Sydney perked up. "Really?"

"Wait up, I'll go with you," Matt said.

Sydney grabbed Matt's arm, and the two of them walked toward the main tent. The moon hid behind thick clouds. Just as Matt and Sydney were about to enter the tent, he felt raindrops on his arm. With the DJ on break, the buzz of student voices bounced off the canvas walls. Matt headed toward the metal tubs for a cold Mountain Dew.

Not much later, Josh unexpectedly entered the tent with Dani. Matt rushed over and high-fived his brother. "I didn't think you'd be back tonight," he said.

Josh looked refreshed, now dressed in street clothes. "Actually, I feel great. It's the best I've felt in a long time."

"No dragon blood to pull you down," Matt said in a whisper.

"Thank God for that ring. But how did you know?"

"When I was in the hospital, I was messing with the ring and it slid open. The sliver of stone from the Human Element was exposed. I knew the stone would kill anything that wasn't human."

Josh looked confused. "Did you know I was the dragon?"

"I didn't. But it makes sense now. Your clothes were shredded the night I thought you were attacked by the dragon, and you had those pellet marks…and the dragon had your blue eyes."

"I can't remember anything."

"I'm not sure I would have killed the animal..."—Matt paused, his voice breaking up—"if I'd known it was you."

"Hey, buddy, looking good," Chad yelled from across the tent.

Josh gave him a thumbs-up.

Sean and Chad darted over. "Man, I can't imagine what you've been through," Sean said.

"The Hulk has nothing on you!" Chad said with a snicker.

Josh hugged his friend. "Don't forget it. Don't get me mad, or I'll fry you alive, then eat you whole."

Chad placed his hands on Josh's shoulders. "That would be true if your brother hadn't killed the dragon part."

Josh smiled. "Yeah, I guess you're right. I'll just have to whup you with my own two hands like always." He grabbed Chad and placed him in a headlock.

Before Chad could give one of his famous quick-witted replies, a sharp voice interrupted their conversation.

"Josh Monroe, this is a Halloween party," Mitzi Martel said with a snort. "Since you're not wearing a costume, you'll have to leave."

The crowd hushed, and everyone's eyes fixated on Mitzi and Josh.

Matt cringed when he heard her high-pitched whine. He'd had enough of the obnoxious girl. "Even though it's none of your business, he *is* wearing a costume," Matt said angrily.

Brittany Benton groaned. "Oh, please... And who's he supposed to be?"

"Your classic American hero!" Matt said, with a bit of pride in his voice.

Chad couldn't resist the opportunity to rattle chains. "I want to know why *you* aren't wearing costumes?"

Mitzi rolled her eyes. "Are you blind? Can't you see we're two witches?"

Chad nodded pompously. "Precisely my point."

The tent filled with rolling laughter. Clearly, most kids within hearing distance agreed with Chad.

"You're disgusting," Mitzi said. As she turned to walk away, the boys heard her ask Brittany, "Have you seen Miss Butterfield?"

Once again, Chad couldn't resist. "She's not coming. She's been delayed...permanently."

Mitzi sneered. "I refuse to talk to such a lowlife."

A heavy downpour earlier that evening had created large pools of water, which collected on the tent's perimeter. This left the canvas sagging at the border. Extra wooden poles reinforced the drooping tent.

Mitzi turned around and assumed her usual pose with nose in the air. "Chad, you're not worth speaking to. You are so beneath us." She hit one of the wooden poles angrily. Either the tent was rotted or heaven intervened, because suddenly the wooden pole tore through the canvas, creating a large gaping hole. In an instant, gallons of fresh rainwater soaked Mitzi and Brittany from head to toe.

The large crowd erupted in applause. The look of mortification on Mitzi's face was hilarious.

Chad stepped in front of both girls as they tried to exit the tent. "Better hurry, girls. You're melting, you're melting..." he screeched loudly and crumpled to the floor like the Wicked Witch of the West in *The Wizard of Oz*.

The entire crowd of teens cheered wildly. The music started up, and no one seemed the least bit upset that Mitzi and Brittany had left the party. Matt thought, *Maybe they weren't so popular after all.*

Dani hugged Josh. "Remind me never to get on Chad's bad side."

Matt watched Zach and Dorie dance to an old Beach Boys tune. *So cool.*

A sad figure stood near the entrance of the tent. Matt motioned to him. Rico Steel looked around and then questioningly pointed to himself. Matt nodded.

Rico slowly approached Matt, who extended his hand and said, "You saved my life."

Rico said, "It was payback for Paragon." Matt gave Rico a one-armed hug as they shook hands.

Rico soon found himself surrounded by numerous members of the Brotherhood.

Matt made as serious a face as he could muster and pulled himself up to his full height. "I talked it over with the other guys, and we want to—"

Rico tried to push past the group, but Chad and Sean blocked his way. "Listen to what the man has to say," Chad said.

Rico was trapped.

"As I was saying, me and the guys want to…want to make you a member of the Brotherhood." Matt actually hadn't discussed the matter with his friends, but a quick glance at them confirmed their approval.

A look of bewilderment filled Rico's face. "I don't know what to say…"

Dani hugged the startled boy. "Just say yes."

Rico grinned. "Yes, yes. After all I've done to you guys, I can't believe you'd let me join."

"Tonight, when the chips were down," Chad said, "you came through."

"Here, here," everyone shouted.

One by one, each member of the Brotherhood gave Rico a fist bump.

Matt's head buzzed. *I guess anything is possible.* He turned to get a can of Mountain Dew from one of the galvanized steel tubs and plowed hard into one of the partygoers. There had to be at least three hundred kids inside the tent, not to mention chaperones.

"I'm sorry," Matt said, reaching out to the person he had just bumped into.

"That's quite all right, young man."

Matt couldn't believe his ears. He looked up, and yes, there stood King Darius. He immediately gave his old friend a big hug. Looking around the tent at all the costumes, Matt said, "I guess you fit right in."

Just then, one of the kids walking past nodded approvingly at the king, and said, "Cool costume. Love the ears."

"Thanks," King Darius said nonchalantly. "I worked on them for hours."

Matt stood in awe. "I can't believe you're here."

"Walk with me," the king requested.

Matt looked over to his brother, whose face expressed how thrilled he was to see King Darius. The king bowed to Josh, who returned the gesture.

Matt followed King Darius outside the tent. He was not surprised to find himself standing in the royal rose garden. Matt found the magic in the world a true wonder.

"Sit with me." Matt joined King Darius on a marble bench.

The ruler's face turned quite serious. "I am sorry it took us so long to realize the amulet was poisoned. It was Madame Violet who first suspected her sister when she discovered Beatrix had left our world and entered the human plane of existence. When it was revealed through our spies that she had procured a teaching position at the academy, alarm bells sounded. Violet immediately enlisted the aid of Dr. Grant to watch her every move."

"Dr. Grant?"

"He's an old friend," the king said. "He confirmed our suspicions. Dr. Grant believed it was Beatrix who broke into the library and stole the books, then blamed him for it."

Matt reached for the amulet. Of course it wasn't there. "Old habits are hard to break," he said timidly.

"I can fix that." The king reached into his pocket and pulled out another amulet. It was more beautiful than the first. "Accept this talisman. I personally guarantee it is not poisoned."

Matt leaned forward, and the king placed the charm around his neck. Matt couldn't hide his excitement. "This is so cool."

The king leaned back and sighed deeply. "As for Damien, he has been apprehended."

Matt sighed. "Thank God… I'm sorry I failed you. I thought I killed him on the mountain."

"You did not fail. Your duty was to recover the Human Element, which you did splendidly. We didn't think you would be able to achieve your goal without killing Damien. But killing Damien was not part of your quest."

"Yes, but won't he start another revolution?"

"I must admit, I had no idea Damien had so many followers. But I do believe we can rest. Any admirers, at least those in high places, have been exposed. What's more, you saved your brother. The blood from the dragon, which entered his body in Paragon, caused a massive metamorphosis."

The king leaned closer to Matt. "I see you figured out the secret compartment in the ring."

"Oh, yeah." Matt slid the ring open to expose the stone.

"You were able to kill the dragon portion without killing Josh, since the Human Element could not harm his human cells. In doing so, you cleansed your brother's body of any trace of dragon blood." King Darius stood. "Walk with me."

"I guess God does help me when I need it."

King Darius led Matt toward the royal palace. "The Eternal does not make mistakes. He knew you before you came into existence. He knew you would serve Him well." He pointed toward the palace. "Some old friends would like to say hello."

Matt looked at the great hall. Just inside the magnificent structure stood two people who waved to him. He recognized them instantly. Matt ran so fast, he almost tripped himself. He wrapped his arms around his old friends, never wanting to let go.

Miss Witherspoon, who was known as Princess Helena in Paragon, squeezed Matt tightly. "I have missed you, Matthew."

His great-grandfather beamed with pride. "Well done, boy."

The king joined the group. "Remember, you can come back anytime," he said.

*How can I do that?* Matt thought.

As though he could read Matt's mind, the king pointed to Matt's right hand. "Use the ring."

Matt sensed himself being pulled away. In an instant, he stood outside the tent with music blasting in the background.

Chad waved his hand in front of Matt. "Yoo-hoo...where've you been?"

Matt smiled. "You wouldn't believe me." He looked around and realized all his friends were there. Zach and Dorie stood together, holding hands. Josh had his arm around Dani's waist, and Sean, Bill, and Chad stood close by with satisfied grins etched on their faces. Even Rico was there. And of course there was Katie. She sauntered up to Matt and gave him a kiss on the cheek.

"You are the best of us," she said, wiping tears from her eyes.

"What's our next adventure?" Chad asked. "It's never boring with you Monroes."

"I think we're good for a while. But I hope I can count on you if something does pop up."

Bill nodded. "We're the Brotherhood. We'll all be here for you."

Matt gave Bill a high-five. "You guys are the best. But can you give me a sec? I need to think."

His friends walked back into the tent, giving him his privacy. The clouds had lifted away, and the full moon lit up the night sky. Matt walked down the lane, admiring the huge maples. He looked up and watched the moon peek in and out through the thinned-out branches. He looked down and kicked the fallen leaves aimlessly. It was a beautiful autumn night. Over a hundred years ago on a very similar night, two children had been murdered in Kingston. *How frightening that night must have been for Nathaniel and Annabelle*, Matt thought. *Now they're at peace.*

Obstacles will always pop up in the future. That is the way of life. But God had blessed Matt with many loyal friends and a loving family. With them at his side, he believed be could defeat any evil. He remembered something King Darius had told him once in Paragon. *Material goods will come and go, but true friends are forever. A man's wealth is not calculated by the number of gold coins in his pockets, but by the number of friends at his side in a time of need.*

Matt felt very wealthy indeed.

# About the Author

Edward Torba is a life-long resident of Latrobe, PA. Ed graduated from the University of Pittsburgh in 1973 and received his Doctorate in Dental Medicine in 1977.

Ed first dabbled in writing while in Dental School, where he developed a children's story about a fictional character, King Molar. Previous publications to his credit are The Magic Trip, Boys Club Guide to Youth Football, and Matt Monroe and The Secret Society of Odontology.

While running a full-time dental practice, Ed works on his Matt Monroe series in his spare time.

For more information and updates on Matt and his friends go to www.edwardtorba.com. To talk with Ed directly, email him at edward.t62@gmail.com

*Payne Mansion, 1901*